P9-EJT-649

D0037814

SPOOK

SPOOK

A "Nameless Detective" Novel

Bill Pronzini

Thorndike Press • Chivers Press
Waterville, Maine USA Bath, England

This Large Print edition is published by Thorndike Press®, USA and by Chivers Press, England.

Published in 2003 in the U.S. by arrangement with Carroll & Graf Publishers, Inc.

Published in 2003 in the U.K. by arrangement with Carroll & Graf Publishers.

U.S. Hardcover 0-7862-5307-X (Mystery Series)
U.K. Hardcover 0-7540-7248-7 (Chivers Large Print)
U.K. Softcover 0-7540-7249-5 (Camden Large Print)

The text of this Large Print edition is unabridged.
Other aspects of the book may vary from the original edition.

Set in 16 pt. Plantin.

Printed in the United States on permanent paper.

British Library Cataloguing-in-Publication Data available

Library of Congress Cataloging-in-Publication Data

Pronzini, Bill.
    Spook : a "nameless detective" novel / Bill Pronzini.
      p. cm.
    ISBN 0-7862-5307-X (lg. print : hc : alk. paper)
    1. Nameless Detective (Fictitious character) — Fiction.
2. Private investigators — California — San Francisco — Fiction.   3. San Francisco (Calif.) — Fiction.   4. Large type books.   I. Title.
PS3566.R67S66 2003
813'.54—dc21   2003041692

For Marcia

PROLOGUE

Hate. Rage.

They'd lived in him for as long as he could remember, like parasites. He'd had them under control until the past year or so. Then they'd begun to feed on all the crap that'd happened to him — feed, grow, become stronger. Now they were bloated things that screamed in his head, burned in his belly, boiled and bubbled in his blood. He slept with them at night, woke with them in the morning, carried them heavy inside him all day, every day. He feared and fought them. Wanted them, clung to them, and knew that someday he'd give in to them.

Here, tonight, they were wild. Howling, hurling themselves at the walls of his mind like a pair of animals in a cage rioting for escape.

Hungry animals, demanding to be fed.

Demanding blood.

Almost there, almost feeding time.

Three A.M. by the dashboard clock. Wet, empty city streets. Trash everywhere. Filth. This was where that hunk of human garbage had ended up. Mind rotted until he was little more than a drooling idiot dressed in rags, stumbling through filth during the day and sleeping in an alley doorway at night. But that wasn't enough punishment for what that bastard had done. He'd gotten away with it too long, left too much wreckage behind. Been free too long. *Lived* too long.

But there'd be justice tonight, by God. Justice! Then both the dead and the living would finally have some peace.

Red light, blinking. He stopped the car and peered at a street sign through the slash of windshield wipers, the thin drizzle. Mariposa Street. The light changed; he turned west, went half a block until he was able to make out the black mouth of the alley. No other headlights on the street, nothing moving anywhere except wind-flung litter. He drove into the lightless tunnel between old buildings.

The reach of his headlamps showed him emptiness, shadow-shapes at the edges and beyond. A little farther, at a crawl now. And the beams outlined the recessed doorway ahead on the right, the huddled mound lying there.

His lips peeled back from his teeth. His head felt huge, as if it were being pumped full of air. But outwardly he was cool and calm. Hands steady, breathing normal, senses sharp as spikes. Like when he was on a hunting trip.

He braked, shut off the headlights but left the engine running. Blackness outside, pulsing red inside. He opened the glove box, took out the six-cell flashlight first, then the Colt Delta.

The gun, clean, oiled, loaded with a full clip, felt cold-hot in his hand; felt good, felt right. His Bushmaster assault rifle, his Micro Uzi, his shotguns were all wrong for the job — too large, made too much noise. His collection of sidearms hadn't included a Colt .41, so he'd gone out and bought one special. The hollow-point ammo, too. Perfect, fitting. Hell, how could he even have thought of using any other kind of weapon?

He stepped free of the car. Wind lashed his face, blew wetness into his eyes as he moved around to the front; he barely felt any of it. Pause to listen. Windsound. Rainsound. Nightstill. He put the flash beam on long enough to get his bearings, then groped blind to the building wall and shouldered along it ten paces to the doorway. He flicked the torch on again, angling it upward to splash white light against the metal door. In the downspill, the mound inside the tattered, grimy sleeping bag lay motionless. He let the beam slide slowly down the door, centered it on the huddled form. Piece of garbage still didn't move.

He kicked yielding flesh. Did it again, harder. Grunt, moan; the body flopped over and the head popped out like a turtle's, the face turned up blind toward him. He'd seen from a distance what time had done to that face, but up close in the flashlight's glare the sight lashed his hate to a frenzy. Ravished, shrunken, blotched and scabbed and wrinkled, but still the same fucking face.

Sounds came out of the gap-toothed mouth, words that weren't words. Then, clear enough, "Who's that? Dot? Who's there, Dottie?"

Dot, Dottie!

He went to one knee, put his face close to the hated face, held the beam to one side so the vague rheumy eyes could see him in the sideglow. "Look at me, you son of a bitch. You know who I am?"

"No, no, Mr. Snow! Oh, oh, Mr. Snow!"

"Not Snow, damn you. Look at me!"

"Luke? Luke?"

He straightened again, kicked the bastard savagely. The screech of pain was like music, high and hot.

"Look at me! *Who am I?*"

Blank stare. "Don't know don't care don't know. You, Luke? You? Never believed you'd do this to me. Oh Dot, oh Luke, oh oh Mr. Snow. Forgive me, Dottie. Give you something bright and pretty. Forgive me? Love me forever?"

He couldn't stand it anymore. Luke, Dot, Mr. Snow . . . he couldn't stand it another second.

He bent, moving the Colt into the dazzle of white.

The hated face stared at it. Saw it or didn't see it, he couldn't tell. Then the face turned down away from him, hid itself in the crossed fold of scrawny arms.

He laid the muzzle close above the right ear and lulled through the trigger.

The recoil threw him up straight again, the light beam dancing crazily within the doorway. He brought the beam back down, steadied it, and when he saw the blood, saw what the hollow point had done to the hated face, it was if taut-strung wires had been released inside his head.

Dead. Finally dead. Finally justice.

He wanted to shout, to laugh. He felt the way he did when he made a quick clean kill in the woods. Killing a man, a hated enemy, a piece of human garbage was no different than putting a bullet in a deer or an elk or a rabbit. Yeah, and so much more satisfying. Justice! Justified!

He located the ejected cartridge case, slipped it into his pocket. Shut off the flash, went back to the car wrapped in wet black. Weapon and six-cell into the glove box. Light up the deserted alley, drive on through and away.

Done, finished. Mission accomplished.

Except for one thing he hadn't counted on. One thing that quickly ate away the pleasure, left him without peace. Scared him.

He was satisfied, but the hate and rage weren't.

Inside they still burned, still boiled and bubbled, still screamed like caged animals.

As if they were still hungry. As if they wanted more.

1

He was the fourth applicant Tamara and I interviewed for the field operative's job. On paper he had all the necessary qualifications and experience, but he didn't make a very good first impression. Not much charisma, for one thing. And he had personal problems.

His name was Runyon, Jake Runyon. Native of Washington state, grew up in Spokane where his father had risen to the rank of police sergeant, lived most of his adult life in the Seattle area. Fourteen years with the Seattle PD, the first seven as a uniformed officer, the last seven working plainclothes on the robbery and then homicide details. Voluntary retirement with a partial disability pension five years ago, reason not set down in his résumé. Since then, until six weeks ago, he'd worked as an operative for Caldwell & Associates, a solidly respectable Seattle investigative agency.

Plentiful professional credentials, but pretty sketchy on the personal side. Except for vital statistics — age 42, height 6'1, weight 190 — Runyon hadn't supplied much information. Moved to San Francisco five weeks ago, in early November; current residence was an apartment on Ortega Street. Evidently he lived alone, since the only family reference he'd included was a terse "no dependents." Shortly after establishing residence, he'd applied for a California investigator's license and had been issued a temporary on the basis of his Washington state license. And that was all.

He showed up on time for his eleven A.M. appointment. Well-dressed in a suit and tie, freshly shaven except for a scimitar mustache, curly brown hair clipped short. He took an inclusive look around the office when he came in, without appearing to do so, the way a good investigator will in new surroundings. He had a crisp handshake and he made and held eye contact whenever he spoke to either Tamara or me. All of that was on the plus side.

On the negative side he looked as though he might have been or might still be ill. He had a large, compact frame and a slablike face, hammerhead-jawed and blunt-angled, like a chunk of quarried stone; but his clothes hung loosely on him, as if he'd recently lost some weight, and the stone slab had an unhealthy grayish cast and seemed to have developed fine cracks and crumbly edges that had nothing to do with age. There was a distance, an inward-turned reticence about him, too, that made him hard to read. For me it was more like confronting a closed fire door than interviewing a man.

He declined a cup of coffee, sat solid and stiff on one of the clients' chairs — a waiting posture that didn't change much throughout the interview. Lot of pressure built up behind that fire door, I thought. If he's not careful, one of these days he'll blow out an artery.

Tamara and I had worked up separate sheets of questions for each applicant. We'd also decided not to compare notes until all the applicants had been interviewed, so as to narrow down the field individually before we did it jointly. That way, we wouldn't be inclined to try to influence each other during the process.

I got the ball rolling with Jake Runyon by asking, "The partial pension — what kind of disability do you have?"

"Far as I'm concerned," he said, "I

don't have any."

"Then why the pension?"

"The department's idea, not mine. All it is is a slight limp, left leg. You notice it when I came in?"

I said, "No," and Tamara shook her head.

"Hardly anyone does, most days. Now and then, when the weather's bad, I get twinges. You might be able to tell then, but you'd have to be paying close attention."

"These twinges —"

"They don't keep me off the job. Or from moving as fast as I always have. I can still run hard if I have to."

"Broken leg what caused the limp?"

"Tibia fractured in three places. Two surgeries to get it fixed right."

"How'd it happen?"

"High-speed chase in pursuit of a fugitive homicide suspect," Runyon said. "A truck hit us and he got away. I came out of it lucky. My partner was driving. He came out of it dead."

"Rough."

"A shame and a waste. But it happens."

"If the leg doesn't cause you problems, why'd you take voluntary retirement?"

"They tried to chain me to a desk after I got out of the hospital the second time. No

16

way. I'm a doer, not a sitter."

Tamara frowned at that, but she made no comment.

I asked, "Any other physical problems?"

"No."

"You look like you might've lost some weight —"

"I'm fine." Through compressed lips.

"Have you had a recent physical exam?"

"Six months ago. My health's good. I'll get you confirmation if you want it."

I let it go. "You went straight from the Seattle PD to Caldwell & Associates, is that right?"

"Right. Interviewed with them before I left the department, to make sure I had a job waiting. You know Caldwell?"

"We've had some minor dealings. Good outfit. You like working for them?"

"Well enough."

"Field work the entire five years?"

"Mostly. Outside interviews, surveillance, bodyguard and security jobs, chasing bail jumpers — you name it."

"Well, we're a much smaller agency, as you can see. Not much surveillance or security work. Mainly we handle skip-traces, insurance claims investigations, background checks. And the occasional offbeat case that nobody else wants."

"All familiar territory," Runyon said. "If anything comes up that I haven't dealt with before, it won't take me long to learn the ropes. I'm a quick study."

I made a couple of notes on his résumé. "Back to Caldwell. Any problems or hassles while you were with them?"

"If you mean black marks on my record, no. Lee Caldwell wouldn't've given me the letter of recommendation if there were."

"I'm just wondering why you left them," I said.

"I wasn't fired or let go. I resigned."

"For what reason?"

Silence. He just sat there, looking halfway between Tamara and me. His eyes, more black than brown, were shadowed.

"Mr. Runyon?"

"My wife died," he said.

Stone-faced and flat-voiced. I might've taken it for a cold response if it weren't for what I saw in those shadowed eyes. For just a second, as he spoke the words, the door opened and I had a glimpse of what lay inside. Grief, suffering . . . emotion so raw and corrosive it was no wonder he had it under such tight guard.

Awkward moment. Tamara and I passed meaningless words of sympathy, the way you do. And she added, "Was it sudden?"

"Yes and no. Cancer. Three months after the diagnosis, she was gone." Pause, and then he said, "Twenty years. You think that's a long time, but it's not. It's the blink of an eye."

Yeah, I thought.

Tamara asked him, "That the reason you quit Caldwell, left Seattle?"

"I couldn't stand it up there afterward."

"Why'd you pick San Francisco?"

"Personal reasons."

"Friends, relatives in this area?" I asked.

"Does it matter?"

"Not unless it has something to do with your work."

"It doesn't," Runyon said. Then he said, in a slow, dragging way as if the words scraped on the membranes of his throat, "My son lives here."

"Son? You say on your résumé that you have no dependents."

"He's not a dependent, he's a grown man with a job of his own." Runyon glanced at his hands, looked stonily at me. "Twenty years," he said again. "Blink of an eye."

"So you moved down here to be near him?"

"More or less."

"Have you applied with any other agencies since you've been in the city?

19

Other jobs of any kind?"

"No. You're the first."

"Getting acclimated, spending time with your son?"

"Getting acclimated. I haven't seen him yet."

"Oh? How come?"

He shook his head, sharply. "Like I said, it's personal. I'd rather not talk about it, you don't mind."

I said, "Suit yourself," but I sensed that at some level he did want to talk about it. The something hidden away behind that door was the lonely man's conflicted hunger for privacy on the one hand, human contact and understanding on the other.

Tamara took over the questioning. "You computer literate, Mr. Runyon?"

"I can operate one of the things."

"Mac or pc?"

"Mac."

"Personal habits. You smoke?"

"No."

"Drink?"

"Not much. Never on the job."

"Recreational drugs?"

"No. I've seen too much of what crack and blow can do."

"Pot?"

"No."

"How do you feel about weed? Same category as hard drugs?"

"No. You want my honest opinion, marijuana should be decriminalized."

"Why?"

"Same reason I think prostitution and all forms of gambling should be legalized," Runyon said. "Trying to legislate morality is a waste of time, money, and manpower."

"Uh-huh. Vice is here to stay."

"Isn't it?"

She said, "You know I'm a new partner in this agency, right?"

"So I gathered from the newspaper ad."

"You mind taking orders from a woman?"

"I don't have any problem with it."

"Black woman just about young enough to be your daughter?"

"No problem with that either. I've worked with women, black and white, young and old. And my partner, the man who was killed in the chase, was black."

"He was driving, you said?"

"The crash wasn't his fault, if that's what you're getting at. I don't hold grudges against dead men, Ms. Corbin. Or live ones, for that matter, black or white."

"So you get along with everybody."

"If they make a reasonable effort to get

along with me. I don't toady to anyone, and I've been known to question authority — male or female — if I think the situation warrants it. Might as well get that said up front. Otherwise, I'm easy enough. And a good investigator. I work hard, I don't object to overtime or scut work, I don't make unreasonable requests, and I don't pad the expense account."

That pretty much ended the interview. Runyon shook hands with each of us again, I told him we'd be in touch one way or the other, and away he went. He hadn't cracked even the ghost of a smile the entire time.

"Mr. Personality," Tamara said.

"Man with problems. But he seemed forthright enough."

"Uh-huh. Working with that dude would be a laugh a minute."

"Like working with me, you mean?"

"You can be pretty funny, specially when you're not half trying."

"Thanks. I think."

"Funny as Drew Carey, sometimes."

Whoever Drew Carey was.

We had a total of nine applicants, and as a matter of course we ran a background check on each one. The check on Jake

Runyon filled in some of the gaps in his personal record. He had problems, all right. A long, sad history of them.

He'd been married twice, the first time at age nineteen to a woman named Andrea Fleming. The following year she'd borne him a son, Joshua. Fourteen months after that, he'd left her for his second wife, Colleen McPhail — a bitter separation and divorce that culminated in Andrea getting full custody of the child and moving to San Francisco, where she'd taken back her maiden name and legally changed the child's surname to Fleming. Evidently her bitterness hadn't been tempered by time; one of Runyon's friends on the Seattle PD told me she'd poisoned Joshua against his father and the boy had grown up hating him, refusing to have anything to do with him. Andrea Fleming had never remarried; had nursed her bitterness with alcohol and died two years ago of liver failure. Runyon's second marriage, meanwhile, had apparently been rock-solid; he worshipped Colleen, the cop friend said. No children from that union, just the two of them together for two decades. And now Colleen Runyon was gone, too, of ovarian cancer, and Jake Runyon was alone except for his estranged son whom he still hadn't seen after five weeks in the city.

Tamara said, "Moved down here looking to patch things up, probably, and he's not getting anywhere."

"Can't be easy finding an antidote to a lifetime of poison."

"Yeah. But the man did it to himself. Left his wife and baby for another woman. I'd be full of poison, too, if a man treated me that way."

"For twenty years? I don't think so. You're not the type who lives in the past, uses booze to nurse an obsessive hatred."

"Might be if I loved somebody enough in the first place."

"As much as Runyon seems to have loved his second wife, you mean?"

"Sure, take his side. Men always stick up for each other."

"I'm not taking anybody's side," I said. "We don't know enough about any of these people to make judgments. All I'm saying is that there are no easy explanations for what people feel or do. Life can be a complicated mess sometimes."

"Ain't it the truth. What Runyon said about twenty years being the blink of an eye — you agree with it?"

"Absolutely. Life itself isn't much more

than three or four."

By the end of the week I had the field narrowed down to two. Jake Runyon was one; the second was Deron Stewart, another ex-cop with similar credentials. Stewart was local, had worked eight years for the San Francisco office of a big national agency. The economic crunch brought about by the sudden collapse of the dot-com industry had cost him his job, but he'd been given an unqualified recommendation and he owned a solid if undistinguished record.

Tamara and I sat down late Friday afternoon to make our final decision. I said, "Two names on my list. There's not much difference in background or experience, so as I see it the choice comes down to personalities."

"Uh-huh."

"How many names on your list?"

"Just one."

"Really? Who?"

"You first."

"Okay. Close call, but my vote goes to Deron Stewart."

She gave me a bent smile. "How come you be picking him?"

"He has a nice, easy way of dealing with

people," I said. "Quick wit, too. And he's upbeat."

"Those the only reasons?"

"Only ones I can think of at the moment."

"Fact that he's African American didn't have anything to do with it?"

"Well . . ."

"You figure I'd be more comfortable working with a brother, maybe?"

"Come on, Tamara, don't bring race into this."

"Me? You the one playing that card, boss man. We been working together four years now, the last two full-time, and you don't know me any better'n that? You think I'm still the hard-ass college kid I was back when?"

She'd been a hard-ass, all right — the type of young urban black who distrusts and dislikes whitey, sees racism lurking in every act and spoken word, and adopts a hostile attitude. The first day she'd walked into this office, to interview for the part-time job of computerizing my old-fashioned operation, she'd worn outlandish clothing, brandished her attitude like a sword, and all but accused me of having ulterior sexual motives toward her. We'd clashed, hard. But there'd been a connection nonetheless, one which allowed us to get past all the crap and give each other a second chance. And she had matured into a person with perspective, tolerance, compassion, a far more adult fashion sense, and a remarkable flair, passion, and professionalism for the detective business. Four years ago it would've been inconceivable to me that I'd one day offer her a full partnership — as inconceivable as making a firm decision to semi-retire at the age of sixty-one.

I said, "Anything but."

"Then don't be patronizing me," she said. There was an edge to her voice, but no real heat. She was making a point, not starting an argument.

"I'm not patronizing you. I was only —"

"You really think Deron Stewart's the best man?"

"Well . . . don't you?"

"No," she said.

"Why not?"

"He's a hound, that's why not."

"Hound?"

"Pussy hound. Didn't you see the way he looked at me, how long he held onto my hand after we interviewed him? Sniff, sniff, sniff, with his big old tongue hanging out."

"Was he that obvious?"

"Was to me. Man's sly, but not so sly a smart woman can't see what he is. He'd be hitting on me inside a week. Be hitting on any other woman he figured might be available, too, black or white, every chance he had."

"You mean while on the job?"

"On the job, off the job, in his sleep. Trust me, he's a hound. I can't work with a hound no matter what color he is."

I like to think I'm a good judge of character, that I can pick up on obvious flaws on a first meeting. Not where Deron Stewart was concerned, evidently. Because he was a black man? Because I'd wanted to believe Tamara would be happier, more comfortable with someone of the same race — patronizing her, as she'd claimed, with reverse racism? Or just because I was getting old and missing signals, more ready for the pasture than I wanted to admit?

She said, "What's the other name on your list?"

"Jake Runyon."

"Right. Only name on mine."

"I thought you didn't much care for Runyon's past or personality."

"Didn't much care for you either in the beginning," Tamara said. "Man's a pro, that's the main thing. I can work with him."

"So are you a pro," I said. "Someday you'll be a better one than I ever was."

"Not better, but just as good." No false modesty in Ms. Corbin.

"So it's Runyon then?"

"Best man for the job. Only one in the bunch worth your time and mine."

I made the call to tell Jake Runyon that he was hired. All he said was, "Good. When do I start?"

2

The phone rang at ten till five, just as I was getting ready to close up shop for the weekend. Tamara was already gone, and I'd been finishing a report on a claims investigation for Western States Indemnity and trying to decide if I should fight the Friday night crowds downtown for a couple of hours of Christmas shopping, or wait until tomorrow and fight the Saturday morning crowds. Tonight might be better, I was thinking, get it over with. It was Kerry's night to pick up Emily and they wouldn't be home until seven o'clock at the latest.

The caller identified himself as Steve Taradash, adding that he was the owner of a company called Visuals, Inc. He'd gotten the agency name out of the phone book, he said, and wanted to know if I was available to "do a small job" for him. He sounded uncertain, possibly a little embarrassed at asking for the services of a detective agency.

"What sort of job, Mr. Taradash?"

"Well, it's kind of difficult to explain over the phone. Could you come here? We're not far from where you are." He gave the address.

"This evening, you mean?"

"If you could manage it. I'll be here until seven or so."

"I'll need some idea of what kind of job you want done first."

"Find out who somebody is. Was."

"I'm not sure what you mean. An identity check?"

"Well, there was an article about it in Wednesday's *Chronicle*. It mentioned us — Visuals, Inc. Maybe you saw it?"

As a general rule I neither read the newspapers nor watch TV news. Investigative work is depressing enough, and I can count on Kerry or Tamara or various clients to keep me abreast of current events. I didn't tell Taradash this; I said only, "I'm afraid not."

"Oh. Well." He made a throat-clearing sound. "The thing is," he said, "I've been stewing about this ever since Tuesday morning. Whether to call somebody or not. I kept hoping the cops . . . police would ID him, turn up some information on his background, but they don't have a clue. He's still a John Doe."

"Who is?"

"Spook."

"Did you say Spook?"

"That's what everybody called him." The throat-clearing sound again. "Look, I'm not very good at this kind of thing, especially on the phone. I've never hired a detective before. Could you come over? Even if there's nothing you can do, I'll pay you for your time . . ."

Five o'clock. Friday evening crowds, Friday evening traffic snarls downtown. Two hours before Kerry and Emily would be home. Visuals, Inc. was more or less on my way to Diamond Heights. And I wouldn't be officially semiretired until after the first of the year.

"Give me half an hour, Mr. Taradash," I said. "I'll let you have the same, free of charge."

Visuals, Inc. occupied half of a converted warehouse on Mariposa, off lower Potrero. The area was semi-industrial, home to all sorts of small businesses, the Municipal Railway bus yards, and the local PBS station, among other things. It was close to downtown, close to the interchange of Highways 101 and 80, close to the Mission

District, Pac Bell Park, S.F. General Hospital.

The centralized location may or may not have much to do with the fact that a fairly high concentration of the city's 8,000-plus homeless population congregates there. The area has a soup kitchen and at least one city-operated shelter, but many of the displaced live on the streets or sleep in squalid little encampments under the freeways and in neighborhood parks such as Franklin Square. Sidewalks, alleys, doorways are littered with shopping carts, refuse, human waste. Conditions aren't as bad as in some other parts of the city, but walking here can be a depressing experience. And I had to hoof it three blocks in a chilly December dusk because street parking is always at a premium, even after five o'clock on a Friday evening. I doled out change to three panhandlers along the way, turned down a fourth because he was drunk on cheap wine and overly aggressive. Life in the city in the new millennium.

The windowless entrance to Visuals, Inc. was locked tight. Plated on the door was a discreet sign with the company's name and nothing else; a bell button was set into the wall next to it, above which another, card-size sign said RING FOR ADMITTANCE. I rang, waited a good two minutes before a voice said, "Yes, who is it?" When I identified myself, chains and bolts rattled and the door opened and I was looking at a guy in his mid-thirties with a severe case of male-pattern baldness and a tic under his right eye that made it seem as if he were winking.

"Steve Taradash," he said. He grabbed my hand, worked it like a slot-machine handle for about three seconds before he let go. "Come in, thanks for coming, I really appreciate it, we'll talk in my office." All run together like that. Nervous guy.

He led me on a fast walk through an areaway into a cavernous space lighted by both spots and fluorescents. Two-thirds of the space contained film-related equipment: cameras, dollies, boom microphones, a variety of wheeled backdrops and a gaggle of furniture and props. The other third was walled off and had two sets of metal doors, above one of which was mounted a presently unlit red light. Sound stage, I thought. Two men were working among the equipment; they paid no attention to us as we passed along the side wall.

At the far end was another closed off section, this one cut up into windowed offices. Two were dark and curtained; the third and largest showed lamplight. That was where we went — Taradash's office. Big, cluttered, evidently soundproofed, and outfitted with a computer, a film projector, another large machine I couldn't identify. The three solid walls were coated with posters, photographs, film stills, and various award certificates, some framed, some fastened to corkboards with pushpins.

Taradash said, "Sit anywhere you can find space," and flopped into a leather desk chair. Two of the other three chairs in there were piled high with miscellaneous stuff. I moved a couple of large cans of film off the third to make room for my hind end.

"What sort of film work do you do, Mr. Taradash?"

He took a cigarette from a pack on the desk blotter. If he'd started to light it, I would have protested; but he didn't. He rolled it between his thumb and forefinger, looking at it with an expression of loathing. "What we are for the most part is an industry supplier," he said. "Rent out equipment to small outfits that can't afford to buy or transport their own — documentary filmmakers, production companies that make indy flicks or commercials. We provide other services, too — sets and a sound stage for indoor shots, film processing, transportation."

"Sounds interesting."

"It can be. Profitable, too — finally. We've been in business seven years, this last one was our best so far and the projection for next year looks even better. You'd be amazed at how much film is shot in the Bay Area, not just the city but within a radius of a couple hundred miles. As much as in L.A., no kidding."

"I believe it," I said.

"Up to my ass in work even this time of year." He blew his breath out, scowled at the cigarette, set it down on the blotter. "Trying to quit," he said. "Bad time to do it, probably, holidays and my workload combined, but I can't take the wheezing and morning cough anymore."

"I know how it is. I used to be a heavy smoker myself."

"You have a hard time quitting?"

"Not really. Cancer scare."

The tic jumped under his eye. "Scares me, too. That, and emphysema. My old man died of emphysema. How'd you do it? Quit, I mean."

"Just gave it up. Cold turkey."

"I can't do that," Taradash said ruefully.

"I tried, a dozen times at least. Patches, inhalers, that gum that releases a chemical makes you sick when you smoke . . . all the damn tricks and none of 'em worked. I'm trying something new this time."

No wonder he was nervous. "New product?"

"No. I'll show you." He produced a penknife from a desk drawer, used the blade to slice the paper lengthwise on the weed in front of him. Then he lopped off the filter, cut the paper and tobacco into little wedges until he had a shredded mess in front of him. He seemed to enjoy doing it; his expression was one of almost unholy glee when he was done. He swept the mess into an ashtray, emptied the tray into his wastebasket. "I do that every time the craving gets too strong — twenty or thirty times a day. Wastes money, but what the hell, I waste it when I'm smoking the goddamn things, right? So far it seems to be doing the job."

"How long now?"

"Five days and counting." He grinned suddenly; it transformed his features, made him look boyish. "Each time I pretend I'm slice-and-dicing one of the tobacco company execs or their frigging lawyers. Very satisfying."

I said I guessed it must be. "About your reason for wanting to hire my agency, Mr. Taradash . . ."

"Spook, right." He shifted through papers, found a clipping and slid it over my way. "The newspaper article I mentioned on the phone, that'll give you some of the background."

The clipping was headed DEATH AND ANONYMITY ON THE STREETS. I smiled a little, wryly, when I saw the byline: Joseph DeFalco. My old pal Joe, one of the last of the old-school yellow journalism hacks. Typically, this story of his was a mixture of straight news reportage, sob feature, and soapbox rhetoric, loaded with bathos and flamboyant metaphor — DeFalco's "personal style" which in fact was loosely patterned on those of Mike Royko and Jimmy Breslin.

Distilled, the facts amounted to these: On Tuesday morning a homeless man in his mid-thirties, known only by the name Spook, had been found shot to death by an employee of Visuals, Inc. in one of their back-alley doorways. He carried no identification, no one seemed to know his real name, and a check of his fingerprints had turned up no match in any state or federal database. Officially he was a John Doe, the latest of more than a hundred and forty John and Jane Does to pass through the medical examiner's office this year.

There was no apparent motive for the shooting. Everyone seemed to agree that he'd been a harmless street person, mentally ill like many of the city's homeless — known as Spook because he had ghosts living inside his head with whom he held regular conversations — but gentle, friendly, nonaggressive. Steve Taradash and his dozen employees had befriended Spook, given him small amounts of money, food, nonalcoholic drinks. One of the employees, a woman named Meg Lawton, described him as "a really sweet man who'd bring us presents sometimes, flowers and little things of no value. He didn't have a mean bone in his body. I just don't understand why anyone would want to kill him."

When I returned the clipping, Taradash said, "You see that part about how many John and Jane Does died in the city this year? How their ashes get scattered if they're not identified?"

"I saw it."

"That's the part really gets me, can't get it out of my head. A man dies and nobody knows his name, who he was, if he was always unbalanced or something made him that way. Scatter his ashes off the Golden Gate and that's it, like he never existed at all. You understand what I mean?"

"All too well," I said.

"Just another crazy street guy. Who cares, right? Well, I do. My people do. We knew him, liked him . . . ah, Christ. I'd really like to know who he was. Contact his people, if he had any. If he didn't . . . maybe arrange for his burial myself." Taradash dragged another cigarette out of the pack, stared at it the way he had at the other one. The tic was working again. "That sound off-the-wall to you?"

"Not at all. It sounds decent, humanitarian."

"Yeah, well, I can afford to be humanitarian. I've made mine and poor bastards like Spook . . . well, you know how it is. The haves and the have nots." He went to work with his penknife again. "Besides," he said, "it's the season, almost Christmas. I always feel sentimental, this time of year."

"Too bad more people don't share your feelings."

"Yeah." The knife point bit deep into his blotter, scoring it. "How long will they keep the body on ice before it's cremated? Thirty days, isn't it?"

"Usually, in a homicide case."

40

"Two weeks till Christmas. You think you could find out who Spook was, something about him, in two weeks?"

"Depends on what kind of leads we can turn up. We've had identity cases that were wrapped up in a few hours, others that couldn't be cleared in two months."

"How much do you charge?"

I gave him the daily rate and the weekly rate, and added the usual "plus expenses." The numbers didn't faze him; he kept right on dismembering the weed.

"So would you be willing to take it on?" he said. "Two weeks, max?"

"Just an identity search? You're not asking for an investigation into the murder?"

"Would that be an extra charge?"

"No. But it might not be do-able. The SFPD doesn't like private investigators mixing into homicide cases. Even if I could get clearance, the odds are I wouldn't be able to find out anything more than they have."

"They can't be making much of an effort. I mean, Spook was just another street crazy to them. And they have a lousy track record with violent crimes anyway. That series in the *Chronicle* a while back . . . the SFPD doesn't exactly inspire confidence these days."

I'd seen those articles, courtesy of Kerry and Tamara. They were the result of a seven-month newspaper investigation into the SFPD and contained some eye-opening statistics: just 28% of serious felonies committed here between 1996 and 2000 solved, the lowest percentage of any large city in the country; only half of all homicide cases cleared; close to 70 percent of robberies and serious assaults not actively investigated by an inspector. The department claimed it was emphasizing crime suppression over crime solution, and I was aware of extenuating circumstances not covered in the paper's exposé and that efforts had been made since to improve performance, but the statistics were disturbing nonetheless. As Taradash had said, they didn't exactly inspire confidence, even in an ex-cop and pro-police citizen like me.

I said, "You have a point, Mr. Taradash. But the police still have resources I can't match."

"So I guess we'll never know who did the shooting."

"If no clear-cut motive emerges, probably not. I take it you have no idea who might have done it, or why?"

"Not a clue. A guy like Spook . . ." He shrugged and wagged his head.

42

"Did he own anything of value?"

"God, no. His clothes were filthy, little better than rags. He never had any money except for what we gave him and what little he could panhandle."

"No trouble or friction with anyone here?"

"My people? Absolutely not. He got along with everybody, we practically adopted the poor bugger."

"Any of your employees spend more time with him than others?"

"Meg Lawton, she's my accountant. She was always talking to him, giving him spare change, feeding him. When he first showed up around here, she caught him taking a leak on the wall next to the loading dock, yelled at him for it. He didn't yell back, like most of them. Told her he was sorry, he'd never do it again, and he never did as far as we know. Next day he brought her a little bunch of flowers that he got somewhere. That's what started us looking out for him, him bringing Meg those flowers."

"When was that, when he first showed up?"

"About six months ago."

"Never saw him in the neighborhood before that?"

"No, never."

"He spend time with any of the other homeless?"

"I don't think so. Pretty much a loner." Taradash finished slaughtering his second cigarette, this one more finely chopped than the first, and dumped the remains into his wastebasket. For a time, then, he looked out into the warehouse. The two workers had disappeared; there was nothing to see out there but stationary objects draped in light and shadow. "Well," he said at length, "there was one guy I saw him with, once. Cold, rainy day and they were sharing a bottle of sweet wine when I came in to work."

"How long ago?"

"Couple of weeks, maybe longer. Right around Thanksgiving."

"Do you know the other man's name?"

"Never saw him before or since."

"Can you describe him?"

"Big, heavier than Spook, three or four inches taller. Dark. Not a black man, but dark. Wore a ratty red and green wool cap pulled down over his ears. That's all I remember."

"Did Spook ever say anything about himself, where he grew up, where he lived before he showed up here — anything at all that might help?"

44

"No. Nothing."

"What did he talk about, aside from begging money and food?"

"He *didn't* beg money or food," Taradash said, "that's the thing. He never panhandled any of us, we always volunteered. As to what he said . . . most of it sounded like gibberish to me. Particularly when he was talking to those ghosts of his. Truth is, I didn't pay a whole lot of attention. Only one who did was Meg."

"They have names, his ghosts?"

"If they did, I don't remember what they were. Meg might be able to tell you."

We'd covered enough ground for now. I'd brought a blank agency contract with me and we got it filled in and signed, and Taradash wrote out a retainer check for three days' work. He said then, "How soon can you start on this?"

"Monday morning, first thing."

"Not tomorrow? I know it's Saturday, but we've got a local commercial scheduled to shoot and I'll be here most of the day. So will Meg and some of my other people."

"Well . . ."

"I don't mind paying extra, if you could manage it."

"That wouldn't be necessary." I thought

it over. Christmas shopping wouldn't take me more than a couple of hours in the morning, and the family outing we had scheduled to pick out a tree wasn't until Sunday. Another couple of hours on the job wouldn't cut too deep into the rest of tomorrow. "I suppose I could stop by," I said. Old Easy Touch. "Say around noon or so."

"I'd really appreciate it," Taradash said. "You don't need to call first, just show up."

He walked me out to the front entrance, shook my hand again with even more enthusiasm. "This takes a load off my mind, I want you to know that. Or maybe I mean eases my conscience. Just being able to do *something*, no matter how it turns out."

I said I knew how he felt. Just being able to do *something* is a major reason I've stayed in this business as long as I have. For a man like me it's one of the job's few nonmonetary perks.

3

On the walk back to the car I saw fewer homeless. Cold night, with a stabbing Pacific wind, and the temperature would drop another ten to fifteen degrees before morning. Many of the displaced were already forted up in shelters or warming themselves with hot meals in soup kitchens; the less fortunate had gone to sit around illegal fires in one of the encampments, or staked out building doorways where they could spread their blankets and sleeping bags. The ones who were still wandering the streets were the hardcore panhandlers and traffic beggars, the Street Sheet newspaper sellers, the drunks and addicts and petty thieves hunting a quick score, the mentally ill like Spook who existed in a twilight world haunted by demons and ghosts.

Every large city in this brave new world has a homeless problem, but San Francisco's seems worse than most. Aggressive sweeps and innovative social service programs have made inroads in alleviating the problem in New York City and Seattle. In my city, however, there is polarization and paralysis caused by guilt, name-calling, political infighting, incompetence, and constant bickering among homeless advocates, the media, neighborhood watchdog groups, the mayor and the Board of Supervisors, and the Department of Human Services. This year alone the city has shelled out well over a hundred million dollars on homeless expenditures. Nobody can agree on an exact figure because accounting procedures are lax; some earmarked tax money just seems to disappear into a bottomless pit. An estimated thirty million alone goes to pay for the jailing of homeless lawbreakers — an average of nearly a thousand arrests per night — and another three million or so for cleanup costs.

Everybody has an opinion, a solution, an agenda: All homeless are needy, disadvantaged folk who should be given aid regardless of who they are; many if not most homeless are part of a disorganized mob of drunks, drug addicts, crazies, criminals, and plain bums who feed off the system like parasites, destroying San Francisco's beauty and damaging its tourist-based economy. Raise taxes to provide more money; quit throwing good money after bad. Sponsor a regional summit on homelessness. Improve conditions in existing shelters; build more shelters as New York City did by rehabilitating 30,000 units of tax-delinquent and abandoned buildings (blithely ignoring the fact that S.F. has little property-tax delinquency and abandoned buildings are virtually nonexistent). Ban panhandling on median strips, use ID cards and fingerprinting to track everyone who uses homeless services. Form a centralized intake system and hold city government agencies responsible for keeping accurate and detailed records of expenditures. Initiate a constitutional amendment to require the state to provide the mentally ill homeless with housing, health care, and food. Stop the free handouts and put the homeless to work clearing up graffiti, repairing vandalized bus shelters, and picking up trash. Set up a twenty-four hour hotline for citizen reports of public drinking, open-air toilet use, drug use, illegal camping, and excessive noise. Create "nautical shelters" by floating some of the fleet of World War II battleships mothballed in Suisun Bay down to the S.F. waterfront, and letting the homeless live on them while performing daily maintenance services.

Good ideas, bad ideas, silly ideas. And meanwhile tempers grew shorter and residents' and visitors' sympathies continued to erode in the face of escalating violence and incidents of public indecency.

My own sympathies lay somewhere in the middle. Compassion for the genuinely disadvantaged — those forced to live on the streets by circumstances beyond their control while seeking to regain a responsible lifestyle, the legion of mentally disturbed turned out of state-funded hospitals during the disastrous Reagan governorship and desperately in need of care and treatment. Zero tolerance for the professional panhandlers, Skid Row drunks, hardline junkies, abusive drifters and home-grown predators allowed to roam free on a city-sponsored, advocate-sponsored mandate. The difference between me and most other taxpayers is that I don't have any easy answers. I want the problem fixed in the best way possible for all concerned, but I lack the knowledge, the tools, the wherewithal to help accomplish the task.

The job I'd just taken on for Steve Taradash didn't make me feel any less frustrated or impotent. The homeless person called Spook was dead; there was nothing I or anybody else could do for him. Identifying him might help to ease Taradash's conscience, but not mine. It meant my taking to the mean streets yet again, dealing with its denizens, and it figured to be a depressing experience no matter what the outcome. I wasn't sure I was up to it.

By the time I got to where I'd left the car, I knew I wasn't up to it. Semiretired, promises to Kerry to back away from shadow-world cases, overload of empathy . . . a nice little bunch of rationalizations, maybe, but there they were. And if I needed one more, it was the fact that it might be necessary to talk to Joe DeFalco, since he'd have compiled a background file for his Spook article, and I was trying to avoid him as much as possible these days. He kept threatening, since I'd made the mistake of telling him about my semi-retirement, to write a feature about me and my career. The last thing I wanted was any more publicity of the hyperbolic variety he indulged in.

So I took the coward's way out. I decided to pass the buck to the agency's brand-new hire.

Jake Runyon was still home when I called his number on the car phone. I jumped right in, saying, "How would you like to start work tomorrow instead of on Monday?"

"I wouldn't mind," he said.

"Time and a half for weekends."

"No problem either way. What's the job?"

"ID and background check on a homicide victim. How do you feel about the homeless?"

"You mean in general?"

"In general, and any specific feelings you might have."

"Some good people, some bad, like any other group. I feel for the genuinely hard-up. The system parasites . . . I can't work up much sympathy. Why? The homicide victim homeless?"

"That's right. You work many street cases for Caldwell?"

"No. They're mainly high-tech and white-collar," Runyon said. "But I spent a lot of years on the down-and-dirty end for the SPD. San Francisco's streets can't be much different from Seattle's."

"Not much, except that the homeless problem here is out of control."

"So I hear. Political hot potato."

"No politics involved in this case. Personal variety."

"Who's paying the bill?"

I told him who and why and as much as I'd learned about Spook from Taradash and DeFalco's article.

"Robbery, grudge motive, or random shooting," he said, "one of the three."

"Probably. Not our concern, though, unless something shakes out during the ID investigation."

"Suits me. I've had enough of that."

"Okay, then. Meet me tomorrow around eleven-thirty at the office. I'll brief you and then we'll head over to Visuals, Inc. and I'll introduce you to the client."

I've had enough of that. Homicide investigation, he'd meant. But I thought that he'd also meant death, enough of death. Amen. I'd had enough of it, too, the professional kind and the personal kind. None in my life as painful as Runyon's recent loss, but a few, such as Eberhardt's, that had been bad enough. Spiritually we seemed to have a lot in common, Jake Runyon and me. Brothers under the yoke.

Kerry said, "You really have turned over a new leaf."

"New leaf?"

"Giving this Spook case to your new man instead of handling it yourself. Isn't it

53

better being home on a cold December night than out on the streets?"

"I've already been out on the streets tonight. And I'd be home now even if I was handling the case. There's no real work to be done until tomorrow."

"You know what I mean. Don't obfuscate."

"Don't which?"

"You also know what obfuscate means."

"Sure do. Wanna obfuscate before dinner?"

"Smart-ass. You think he'll work out all right?"

"Who?"

"Jake Runyon. He sounds like a man with problems."

"Everybody's got problems," I said. "He's dealing with his the best he can. Besides, he's a pro. Tamara was right — best man for the job."

Kerry pulled a face. "I can't believe you wanted to hire a black man just because you thought it would make her happy."

"That wasn't the only reason, I told you that. Deron Stewart's qualifications —"

"— weren't quite as good as Jake Runyon's. Which you also told me. Sometimes you try so hard to please, you don't think things through."

"Yeah," I said.

"You might have really offended her."

"She wasn't offended."

"But she might've been."

"Might've been doesn't count. She wasn't."

Kerry said musingly, "She's only twenty-five."

"So?"

"I wish I'd been that smart and insightful at her age."

"And you wish I was now, at my age."

"I didn't say that."

"Didn't have to. Anyhow, you're right. By the time she's sixty-one she'll probably have gone national, head up a dozen branches and be a multimillionaire."

"Well, I wouldn't be surprised. She has that kind of potential."

"Whereas I never did."

"I didn't say that either. Are we feeling a bit gruffly tonight?"

"No, we're not. Not if we don't spend the evening picking on us."

"If only you weren't so pickable," she said. Her face was straight, but her eyes said she was yanking my chain a little. All the women in my life — Kerry, Tamara, even Emily — seemed to take an unholy joy in deviling me now and then. The reason for it escaped me. Pickable. What makes somebody pickable, anyway?

We were in the living room with a wood fire going, white wine for her and beer for me. Emily was in her room with Shameless the cat, her door shut and locked; she'd disappeared in there as soon as she and Kerry walked in. Fast hug, peck on the cheek, and she was gone. I figured she was either working on her costume for her school's Christmas pageant next week, or wrapping presents. She'd been carrying a big sack and wouldn't let either of us see what was in it.

I drank some of my beer-flavored water. New Year's resolution: Start treating myself to a better quality of beverage. The stores were full of local microbrews, among them some hoppy IPAs that people kept touting to me.

"Did you find out what Emily wants for Christmas?" I asked.

"Yes, she told me. Her fondest dream wish . . . her words."

"And?"

"Her own cell phone."

"What? At her age?"

"A lot of kids have them now."

"Ten-year-olds going around ringing and yacking in public? Who do they talk to?"

"Friends, family. It keeps them connected."

"Connected," I said. "When I was a kid, we didn't need to be jabbering on the phone to feel connected."

"Did they have telephones when you were a kid?"

"Hah. Funny."

"Well, you sound like an old fogey."

"Maybe I am. But most people of my generation . . . our generation . . . turned out just fine without portable phones and pagers and handheld computers and all the other techno gadgets they have nowadays."

"Times change, darlin'. Lifestyles change. Kids grow up a lot faster, and there's a greater need for connection. It's anything but a kind and gentle world out there, as I don't have to tell you. Cell phones aren't just for kids' amusement, they're for emergencies too. And to keep emergencies from happening."

No way I could argue with that. "Okay," I said. "Still, those things are expensive."

"The one Emily wants is reasonable enough."

"You mean she's got a specific brand all picked out?"

"Oh, yes. The same kind Carla Simpson has. Nokia 3360, AT&T model. It comes with battery, charger, and headset, but she's also lobbying for a couple of accessories."

"What kind of accessories can a cell phone have?"

"A leather carrying case with belt clip, for one. And . . . let's see . . . an extra face plate in either polar blue or vesuvius red."

"My God." I took another hit of watery beer. "Just how much does all of that cost?"

"Under two hundred dollars."

"*Under* two hundred. A bargain."

"It's not bad, really, at today's prices. And it's the only thing she's asking for. I thought if you'd get the equipment, I'd pay the monthly rate for six months. If she doesn't abuse the privilege, and consents to doing a few extra chores, then she can keep it for another six months. And so forth on that basis."

"So you really think we ought to do this."

"Well, it'll grant her wish and teach her care and responsibility at the same time. Why not indulge her a little?"

I thought it over. Kerry was right. After all Emily had been through in her young life, the tragic loss of both her birth parents and the knowledge that they'd been living a double life, and the restructuring of her entire existence, she was entitled if any ten-year-old was. For the first few months she'd been with us, even though she'd wanted the adoption as much as we did, she had been frightened, withdrawn — a state worsened by a shooting incident that had nearly cost me my life. Lately, with both my life and our home life back on an even keel, there'd been positive signs that she was emerging from the crisis period, like a butterfly from its cocoon. She had started to make friends among her classmates at her new school — she and Carla were inseparable these days — and her grades were improving as well. She smiled more often, was more communicative. And she'd stopped sleeping with all the lights on in her room.

"Okay," I said, "so we'll play extravagant Santa this year. As long as she doesn't expect to get expensive gifts every Christmas."

"I don't think she will."

"What was that model number again?"

"Nokia 3360."

"Right. Charger, headset, carrying case, and, uh, red or green face plate."

"Vesuvius red or polar blue. And the charger and headset are included with the phone. You'd better write it all down."

"I'll remember."

"No, you won't. Write it down."

"Later," I said. "Now, how about you?"

"How about me what?"

"What do you want for Christmas, little girl?"

She smiled, then got up in that languid way of hers and came over and plunked herself down on my lap. "I already have everything I want, Santa," she said.

"Is that right?"

"Yes, that's right. I'm content."

"Must be something you need or would like."

She wagged her auburn head. "Your turn. What do you want for Christmas?"

"You to stop picking on me."

"I don't know, that's a pretty tall order. What else?"

"Easy. You for the rest of my life, just like this."

"Snuggled up in your lap?"

"Until my bones get too brittle to support the weight."

"Well, I guess that's do-able. Say another thirty years' worth?"

"I'd settle for twenty."

"Thirty, minimum," she said and kissed me.

The kiss started out light and tender, but it didn't stay that way for long. Never does with Kerry and me. We went at it enthusiastically for awhile, hanging on tight, before we came up for air.

And there was Emily, grinning at us from ten feet away.

"Boy," she said, "you guys. Carla's parents don't do *that* anymore and they're a lot younger."

"Is that so," Kerry said. "How do you know they don't?"

"Carla told me."

"And how does she know what her folks do when she's not around?"

"She heard them talking once in their bedroom. Arguing, I guess. Her mom said she was glad it happened because she was tired of being pestered all the time."

"Glad what happened?"

Emily said matter-of-factly, "Her dad can't get it up anymore. But don't tell anybody, it's supposed to be a secret," and then went skipping off into the kitchen.

Kerry and I looked at each other. She sighed and got slowly off my lap.

"Kids," she said.

"Yeah," I said.

There didn't seem to be anything else to say.

4

Tamara

Horace laid his Christmas surprise on her that night at dinner, two weeks early.

Long day and she didn't feel like going to a restaurant, just wanted to veg out in front of the TV with the rest of last night's pizza. But he kept after her till she finally gave in. He had the fidgets, even worse than the past few nights. Excited and nervous at the same time — always a sure sign there was something worrying around in that big head of his.

So they went over to the Grotto on Lake Street, a couple of blocks from their flat on 27th Avenue. Usually Horace had a pint or two of IPA — man did love his beer — but tonight he ordered scotch, neat. Uh-oh, Tamara thought. Scotch meant this was a Big Deal; Scotch meant she would either love or hate whatever it was he was fixing to tell her.

He didn't waste any time. Slugged down half his drink soon as it came, leaned forward with his eyes all shiny, and covered her hands with both of his. He had the biggest hands. Soft hands. Slow hands that made her shiver every time he touched her, specially in bed. Large all over, that man. Two hundred and fifty pounds of dynamite, he'd said to her once, with a two-inch fuse. Hah. Two times four, just about.

"Baby, I have news. Major news."

"Already figured that much."

"I had an audition today. At the conservatory."

"Audition?"

"With a symphony conductor. Mr. Davalino arranged it, had me play movements from two of the six *Suites for Cello* by Bach and Tchaikovsky's *Peter Ilyitch*." Big grin. "It went fine. The conductor said my *sostenuto* was the best he'd heard in a young cellist."

"*Sostenuto*. Singing tone, right?"

"Right. If everything goes well now . . . just what I've been working for, praying for. A seat with a major orchestra."

"Oh, baby, that's wonderful." His excitement had flowed into her; she squeezed his hands. "But why didn't you tell me about the audition? Must've been set up for a while. Auditions don't just happen all of a sudden."

"Two weeks. That's why I've been so stoked lately. I should've told you, I know, but I . . . well, I was afraid of jinxing it."

"Mr. Superstitious. Okay, never mind. Wouldn't be the S.F. Symphony, would it? You tell me that, I'm liable to wet myself."

"No, but almost as good." The grin flickered. He took another hit of his Scotch. "The conductor, Mr. Greenbaum, and his orchestra manager came up from L.A. just to hear me play."

"L.A. Philharmonic?"

"No. They were there to see somebody about a donation. Mr. Greenbaum doesn't usually do field auditions, but he's an old friend of Mr. Davalino. They were at Juilliard together."

"Juilliard. That's in New York."

"Yes, but that's not where he lives now."

"Well, where does he live? Where's his symphony?"

"Philadelphia."

The excitement cooled in her. "Philadelphia," she said.

"He needs a cellist for their spring season. He wants me to start practicing with the orchestra right after the first of the year. All expenses paid for two weeks.

64

If he and the principal cellist are satisfied, and he thinks they will be, the seat is mine."

She didn't say anything.

"Baby, don't look like that. This doesn't mean I'm leaving you."

"What else would you call moving to Philadelphia?"

"You don't understand. I want you to go with me."

Silent again. She wanted to pull her hands away, but she didn't do it. Just sat there letting him hold on, looking at her all earnest and eager out of those fierce eyes of his. Two hundred and fifty pounds, ugly as sin . . . how could a man who looked so mean be gentle as a lamb, play classical music like an angel?

"Tamara, listen . . . I'm asking you to marry me."

The words seemed to echo in her ears. She listened to the echo, let its meaning sink in — and burst out laughing. Couldn't help it. Laughter just came rolling out, low and raw in her throat.

It hurt him, she could see that, but at the moment she didn't care. He said, "What's so funny? I've never been more serious. We never talked much about marriage —"

"Why spoil a good thing. Uh-huh."

"I never said that."

"No. I said that. Still saying it."

"If I'd proposed earlier, you'd have said yes. I know you would have."

"Then you know wrong."

"It's not just because of Philadelphia that I —"

"Like hell it's not. Word marriage wouldn't have come into your head, much less out your mouth, if it wasn't for that symphony seat and we both know it."

Now he was flustered. "Yes, it would have . . . I wanted to ask you a dozen times but I was afraid you . . . Tamara, listen. I love you and you love me. That's all that really matters, isn't it?"

Everybody said there wasn't any such thing as love at first sight, but she'd loved Horace from the first minute she set eyes on him — in psych class, opening day of the fall semester at S.F. State five years ago. Shamed her a little to think how aggressively she'd pursued him; to remember the fool thing she'd said to him the first time they went to bed, "Lord, I wish I was still a virgin for you." They'd lived together four years now and she believed she knew him so well, as well as she knew herself.

Wrong, Tamara. Nobody knows anybody, including themselves.

66

"*Isn't* it all that matters?" he said again.

"No."

"What're you saying? You're not turning me down?"

"I'm saying I don't want to go Philadelphia with you, married or unmarried."

"Your career? Is that the reason?"

"Pretty good reason."

"Baby, there're plenty of detective agencies back east. Or . . . another profession, one with better opportunities. With your computer skills —"

"What's wrong with detective work?"

"Nothing. I'm only saying —"

"You're saying start over, doesn't make any difference what the job is. Well, it does make a difference. I told you enough times how much I like what I'm doing, how much a full partnership in the agency means to me. As much as being a concert cellist means to you."

"I understand that, but —"

"No you don't, not if you think I'll just drop everything and walk out on the man after all he's done for me, give up my chance to be my own boss — quit being Tamara Corbin and be Mrs. Horace Fields in fucking Philadelphia."

"Shhh! People are staring at us."

She glowered at him. "Let 'em stare."

"All right," he said. "All right, maybe I was being a little insensitive —"

"A little!"

"I understand, baby, believe me I do. It's just that the prospect of playing with a major symphony orchestra . . ."

"Sure. Lot more important than being a private eye, right?"

"No. No! That's not it at all."

"Sounds like it to me."

His face got all scrunched up like a tantrumy kid's. "Don't be like this. We can work this out, I know we can."

"How? Get married and live three thousand miles apart, see each other for a weekend every few months? This child's not made that way, you hear what I'm saying?"

"If you love me —"

"What's *that* now? Try to make me feel guilty?"

"No . . ."

"If you love me you'll go to bed with me. If you love me you'll give up your career and move to Philly with me. Make the big sacrifice. That's emotional blackmail, my man. That's bullshit."

She could feel tears in her eyes. Tough Tamara Corbin, cop's daughter, hip-hop girl, never took crap from anybody, hadn't cried since she was about eight years old — and here she was about to bawl her eyes out in a public place. She jerked her hands away angrily. Looked off from him, across the crowded restaurant at nothing . . . at something that swam into focus.

Christmas tree. Tall, lots of lights and tinsel, angel in a gold and red dress stuck up on top. Pretty, like the ones the folks used to have when she and Claudia were growing up. She'd always loved this time of year. Didn't even care that all the trappings were for white family holidays, not black family's. Carols, decorations, Santa Claus, sappy movies, Christmas eve, presents on Christmas morning . . . loved everything about it. All those Christmases in Redwood City, four fine ones since with Horace, and now this year . . . the 25th was less than two weeks away and she'd really been looking forward to . . .

The lights on the restaurant tree blurred to misty yellow and red and blue halos. Ready to start bawling now. Except that she couldn't. Wouldn't. Not here. Not anywhere, dammit, not over a damn man.

"I can't stay here," she said. "I'm going home."

". . . You're right, it's better if we talk this out in private —"

"Nothing to talk out."

Got up without looking at him, hurried away through the tables to the front entrance. The woman at the cashier's desk said, "Merry Christmas," as she passed by, but Tamara barely heard her and didn't answer.

5

I was a few minutes late for the eleven-thirty meeting with Jake Runyon. Saturday mornings, downtown, in mid-December are a madhouse: clogged Sutter-Stockton Garage, clogged streets, clogged sidewalks, clogged stores. Piped Christmas music and sharp-elbowed shoppers chased me around Macy's, which turned into an adventure in frustration. Macy's didn't sell the Nokia cell phone and accessories Emily coveted, they didn't have Kerry's favorite perfume or any jewelry I liked well enough to buy for her, they didn't have anything I thought would appeal to Tamara. I went up to the women's clothing department and wandered around looking at garments and trying to imagine them draped around Kerry's slender body or Tamara's rounder one. Nothing there, either. Next stop, the lingerie department. Poking around in there made me feel vaguely like a fetishist; I slunk away after ten minutes without buying anything.

By this time it was ten after eleven and I'd had enough of shopping. How women can spend an entire day — hell, entire weekends — in malls and stores is beyond my understanding. Two hours of crowds, noise, indecision, and dissatisfaction was at least an hour past my endurance limit. Presents for the three women in my life could wait until I had time to hunt up a store that specialized in cell phones and another one or two that would solve the gift dilemma for Tamara and Kerry. I might even take Kerry at her word that she already had everything she wanted and forgo a present for her entirely . . . No, I wouldn't. Not if I expected to enjoy the privilege and pleasure of marital relations during the first three months or so of next year.

Runyon was waiting in his car when I finally got to O'Farrell Street. The car was typical of the man: a strictly functional dark gray Ford sedan with several years and no doubt a lot of miles on it, and still bearing Washington state plates. I said I was sorry for being late; he waved the apology away. "I'm used to waiting," he said. "I didn't even notice the time." Also typical of the man, as I was learning.

We went upstairs and I briefed him on

the relevant points I'd noted during Friday evening's interview with Steve Taradash. He asked a few cogent questions, wrote down the answers in a notebook not unlike the one I carry. The questions were tersely worded; he didn't have anything to say that required more than a couple of sentences, and nothing at all that wasn't business related.

I had him fill out and sign a form for the bonding company, so he could be added to the agency bond. Then I gave him one of the spare keys to the office. Tamara would have to decide if he should be granted access to her computer files; not my department.

Downstairs, I asked if he wanted to ride over to Visuals, Inc. with me. He said no, politely, he'd follow me in his car, save me the trouble of having to bring him back. Half-truth, I thought. He didn't care to ride with me because it would've meant small talk, establishing a connection in an enclosed space. Nothing personal against me; it was a loner thing, part of that reticence of his. Hard man to read, to talk to one on one. He preferred to deal with people, professionally and otherwise, in ways that were glancing, impersonal.

I wondered if he'd been that way before

the loss of his second wife. At least partly, I decided. He was the kind of man who let few individuals get close to him, who for the most part reserved his inner self for someone he loved, trusted, connected with on a deep private plane. He and the second wife must have made a very close, self-contained unit — two people moving through life as if in a thinly membraned bubble, venturing out separately for practical purposes but neither of them whole unless they were together. People who didn't need many friends or outside activities, who found complete fulfillment in each other.

I understood that kind of man, that kind of relationship. Essentially Kerry and I were like that, even more so before we let Emily inside our little bubble. If I lost her, as Runyon had lost his wife, would I be as he was now? Almost certainly. Half a unit — half a man. Existing for my work and little else, except for Emily in my case as Runyon's estranged son was in his.

Brothers under the yoke, all right. In more ways than one.

Parking in the Franklin Square vicinity was as bad on Saturdays as it was during the week. I let Runyon have the first space I saw, then had to drive around for ten minutes before I found another spot a couple of blocks off Mariposa. Getting my exercise whenever I came here.

Steve Taradash, contrary to his assurances, was absent from Visuals, Inc. Some sort of urgent business, the guy who admitted us said; he was due back at one o'clock. The guy pointed us toward Meg Lawton's office with a mild warning to keep out of the way of the "shoot." This translated to a film crew busily setting up cameras and equipment and wheeling sets and props around in the vicinity of the sound stage. All the hectic activity drew my attention as we walked to the offices, but not Runyon's; he might have been alone in the building, eyes front all the way.

Meg Lawton greeted us enthusiastically. She was a large, fiftyish bottle blonde with a nurturing smile belied by sad blue eyes: earth mother in turquoise polyester, a little careworn and disillusioned, but clearly still clinging to her own set of youthful ideals.

"I'm so glad Steve called you," she said. "What happened to that poor man . . . Spook, I mean . . . well, it's awful. Just awful."

I said, "You do know we're not investigating the homicide."

"Yes, I know, just trying to identify him. The police haven't found out a thing so far. I don't suppose they'll ever find out who killed him in his doorway."

"His doorway?" Runyon said. "He always slept in the same spot?"

"Yes, once he knew we — Steve, I should say — had no objections."

"Always alone?"

"Oh, yes, always."

"You ever see him with anyone during the day?"

"Other homeless people, you mean?"

"Anyone at all."

"No. Except for his ghosts, of course . . . he was always talking to them."

I asked, "Do you know a homeless man, big, dark, wears a tatty red and green wool cap?"

"Big Dog? I don't know him, no, but I've seen him, heard the name."

"From Spook?"

"No, from another homeless person. Spook wouldn't have had anything to do with Big Dog, I'm sure."

"Why wouldn't he?"

"He just wouldn't," she said. "Spook was friendly, very polite . . . such a gentle soul. And Big Dog . . . well, he's the exact opposite. An ugly personality, if you know what I mean."

"Not exactly, Mrs. Lawton."

"I don't like to speak ill of the disadvantaged, but Big Dog . . . he's an angry man. Very aggressive, foul-mouthed. I've only seen him twice and he was screaming obscenities at someone both times."

"Not Spook?"

"No. He wasn't around either time."

"Mr. Taradash mentioned seeing them together once, around Thanksgiving," I said. "Sharing a bottle of cheap wine in a doorway."

"Really? Spook and Big Dog? Steve never told me that."

"So evidently they did know each other, spent some time together."

"I suppose so. Well, I shouldn't be surprised. Spook spent some of the spare change we gave him on wine, there wasn't anything to be done about that, and if Big Dog knew Spook had alcohol he'd demand a share. And Spook would've given it to him willingly, that's the way he was."

"Violent, this Big Dog, would you say?" Runyon asked.

"Oh, yes. But if you're thinking he's the one who shot poor Spook, no, I don't think so."

"Why not?"

"A man like that wouldn't have a gun."

"Why wouldn't he?"

"He's an alcoholic," Meg Lawton said. "Drunk both times I saw him. And his clothes are filthy, just rags. If a homeless man like that ever had a gun, he'd have pawned it for money to buy liquor."

"Unless he used it to get money another way."

"You mean . . . robbery?"

"Armed robbery, that's right."

"But that's . . . no, I don't believe that. Besides, what possible reason could he have for killing Spook? That poor man didn't have anything worth stealing, no money or valuables. He spent whatever anyone gave him on . . . well, what were essentials to him." Meaning wine and tobacco.

"You're sure of that, Mrs. Lawton?"

"Absolutely," she said. "If Spook owned anything of value, I'd have known it. We were friends. Really, I'm not just saying that. I was his friend and I think he felt the same about me." She pushed her jaw out a little and said again, "I'd have known."

"If this Big Dog had some kind of grudge against him," Runyon said, "would you have known that?"

"I think so. I think he'd have said something. He was always talking to his ghosts about people on the street. Some of it didn't make much sense — he was disoriented a lot of the time — but sometimes you could understand the gist of it. I never heard him say a bad word about anyone, or mention any trouble."

"Where does Big Dog hang out, do you know?"

"Over in the Square, probably," she said. "That's where he was the two times I saw him."

"Franklin Square," I explained to Runyon. "Park a couple of blocks from here — we passed it coming over."

He nodded. "The other street people Spook talked about, Mrs. Lawton — any names you can remember?"

". . . Delia, Mac something, Pinkeye. There were so many . . ."

"Anything specific about any of them?"

"No, I don't think so. Nothing that made any sense."

"What about his life before he showed up here?" I asked. "He ever say anything about that?"

"I'm not sure. Little things now and then . . ."

"Names, places?"

79

"The only one that sticks in my mind is Sweetwater Street. I think it might be where he lived once. He didn't say so, but that was the impression I got."

"No such street in the city."

"I don't have any idea where it might be," she said. "It was one of his lost days when I heard him say it . . . you know, when he wasn't tracking very well."

Runyon asked, "What can you tell us about those ghosts of his?"

"Well, he had conversations with them. Long, strange conversations that didn't make much sense." She paused, frowning. "One time I heard him say 'Are you still mad at me, Dot? I'm sorry for what I done, you know I'm sorry.' And then he started to cry. That poor, sick man . . . he cried like a baby."

" 'Dot.' That was one of the ghosts' names?"

"Yes. A woman, definitely. Another time it was 'Dot honey.' It seemed to hurt him somehow, whenever he said her name."

"As if there was a painful memory attached to it?"

"Yes. Exactly."

"What about the other ghost? Or were there more than two?"

"Three, I think. I'm not sure."

"The one you are sure of, man or woman?"

"Man. Luke, or it could have been Duke."

"And the third?"

"Sometimes he'd say things like 'No, no, Mr. Snow.' And 'Ain't that so, Mr. Snow.' Always rhyming it."

"Just Mr. Snow, no other name?"

"Just Mr. Snow."

"Dot, Luke or Duke, Mr. Snow. Real people who died, you think, or just figments?"

"Well . . . I'd say real people. Anyway they were to him."

"Assuming they were real," I said, " 'Dot honey' indicates someone close to him. Wife, girlfriend, sister."

"That was my impression, too."

"Did you get any idea of what he did to her or thought he did to her?"

"No, none."

"Or of who either of the men were, what relationship he might have had with them?"

Sad shake of her head. "I'm not being much help, am I?"

"On the contrary, Mrs. Lawton. You're doing fine."

We asked her a few more questions,

none of which produced any potentially useful information. It was well past one o'clock when we were done and Steve Taradash still hadn't put in an appearance. Most of the other employees were involved with the film shoot, so questioning them would have to wait. Runyon asked Meg Lawton to show us the doorway where Spook's body had been found. She led us through a back door onto the loading dock, down concrete steps into a wind-blown, litter-strewn alley.

"We try to keep the area back here clean," she said apologetically, as if the alley's state was some sort of social lapse, "but with so many homeless, and the careless way people throw things out of cars . . . it's just an impossible job."

Neither Runyon nor I had anything to say to that. We were both taking visual impressions of the alley as we followed Mrs. Lawton along the warehouse wall. It was wide enough to allow room for a small truck to back into one of the dock's two loading bays — almost wide enough to be called a street. Down at the far end, a raggedy homeless man was poking among the contents of an overflowing shopping cart; otherwise it was empty of people, if not of parked vehicles. The buildings on both sides made it into a canyon where the wind played swirl games with newspapers, food wrappers, the remains of a cardboard carton.

"This was Spook's doorway," Meg Lawton said.

It was about fifty feet east of the loading dock and fifty yards or so from the nearest cross street, Hampshire. Narrow space, not more than five feet wide, which would make it cramped sleeping quarters; but deep enough so that it afforded some shelter from the elements. On the rough pavement were dark stains that someone — Mrs. Lawton, maybe — had tried and failed to eradicate with a brush and an abrasive solvent.

The door there was metal and appeared to be secure. Runyon asked, "What's on the other side?"

"A supply room. The only time the door is opened is when there's a delivery."

"The person who found the body — is he working today?"

"Verne Dolinsky, one of our warehousemen. No, he's off today."

"Be here on Monday?"

"Yes, but he's a new man, only with us a short time. He didn't know Spook as well as the rest of us." She was hugging herself, staring down at the stained pavement. A little shudder went through her. "It's freezing out here. If you're done . . ."

"Jake?" I said. "Anything else?"

"Not right now."

Back inside, we found Taradash finally back from his urgent meeting. I introduced him to Runyon, told him Jake would be handling the field part of the investigation. Taradash had no objection once I assured him that our entire agency worked as a team, no additional charge.

Runyon asked how long the filming would last, if it was all right if he stopped back later to talk to some of the other employees. Taradash said sure, any time, and requested that we leave by the loading dock door because of the shoot. On the way back there I said to Runyon, "Blue collar boys, that's us. Tradesmen please use the rear door."

Feeble joke and he didn't crack a smile. But then, the funniest man alive would have had trouble getting a smile out of Jake Runyon these days. We both remained silent until we were outside and on our way through the wind-chilled alley.

"You want to take over from here, Jake?" I said then.

"Counting on it. See if I can locate this

84

Big Dog for starters."

For no good reason I said, " 'And when the big dog comes home, he'll tell you what the little dog's done.' "

"Come again?"

"Line from an old jazz song. 'St. Louis Blues.' "

"You a jazz fan?"

"Most of my life. But I don't pay as much attention as I used to."

That was enough small talk for him. He pulled his collar up tight around his throat and said, "One question. You have contacts with the SFPD?"

"I know a couple of guys on the Bureau of Inspectors."

"I'd like a look at the official report, just for background. Will one of them let me see it? Talk to me about their investigation?"

"Answer your questions, at least."

"Let me have a look at the body?"

"Shouldn't be a problem."

"Who do I ask for first?"

"Jack Logan. Lieutenant. I've known him the longest — we used to play poker together. The other man is an inspector, Harry Craddock. If you need me to verify your employment, I'll be home the rest of today." I passed over one of the business cards with my home number on it. "Feel free to call yourself, any time, any reason."

"Thanks, but I don't think it'll be necessary."

We parted on Hampshire Street. No more words, just a nod from Runyon before he moved away, walking fast and ramrod-straight with his hands stuffed in the pockets of his overcoat.

He was a hard man to like as well as a hard man to know, unless you were cut from similar cloth. I wasn't sure I liked him much, at least not yet, but I was pretty sure I understood him and could work with him. Time would tell if Tamara, as young and high-strung as she was, felt the same.

6

Jake Runyon

Back in his element.

Little twitches of life in him again.

Funny way to feel, walking among the homeless and the derelicts shivering in the gray cold of Franklin Square. But you couldn't control something like that. He'd been numb for so long, ever since Colleen died. No, before . . . from when the chemotherapy hadn't done any good and hope faded and he'd been forced to face the fact that he would lose her. So numb he could barely function, walking around like a zombie — days and nights of the living dead. So numb after she was gone he couldn't even lift his .357 Magnum, much less shove it into his mouth and eat it. Three nights of that, three nights of sitting numb and sweat-soaked with the gun as heavy as a slab of granite on his lap before he'd faced another fact: he didn't want to die yet. That had numbed him even more, because the desire to live seemed like a betrayal of Colleen, a mockery of her suffering.

The decision to leave Seattle, the move to San Francisco, the attempts to contact Josh . . . all done numbly. Even the need for work, something to occupy his time and thoughts, had been a dull need motivated more by inactivity than desire. The job application and interview, the call saying he'd been hired, the second call putting him to work on this Spook business — none of it had made him feel any less empty. Numb this morning, numb at the agency office, numb at Visuals, Inc. It wasn't until he'd left Bill and walked over here that he'd begun to regain some awareness, to *feel* again. For the first time he was smelling this city, the dank effluvium of its streets. Feeling the cold, tasting the salt in the wind. Just vagrant twitches of his senses, but sharp enough to cut through the numbness. Like when you woke up with your arm asleep and for a while you couldn't lift it or move your fingers and then all at once the tingling started, little pinpricks of life returned.

He knew this kind of urban environment, maybe that was part of it. The streets, the down-and-out who lived on them, the predators who hunted on them. Seattle or San Francisco or any city you could name, it didn't make any real difference. The streets and the people were essentially the same. His element, no question. He was at his professional best out here on the squalid sidewalks, the needle- and bottle-strewn gutters. He'd been away from the streets too long, hadn't really worked them since his days on the Seattle PD before the car smash that had killed Ron Cain. The Pike's Market area downtown, before they cleaned it up; West Seattle and the railyards and the terminals along the East Waterway and the Duhamish Waterway. His beat. His dirty little world.

The five years with Caldwell & Associates had made Colleen happy, but not him. White-collar work in better neighborhoods, among the middle-class and the gentry. Mostly safe, and mostly without either challenge or any real satisfaction. Much smaller agency here, operating out of far less opulent quarters than Caldwell's, and just two people to answer to — a mismatched pair, if he'd ever seen one, but even so a business relationship that seemed to work. Maybe this Spook case was atypical of the kind of jobs that came their way; could be he'd end up handling the same type of mostly boring, by-rote investigations he'd been given at Caldwell. And maybe not. Bill had been in the game a long time, public and private both, and he'd had his share of dealings with rough trade; you could tell it by the questions he asked, the way he handled people, and you could see it in that craggy, beat-up face of his. Solid rep, and willing to take on a lowdown case like this one, the kind the bigger agencies like Caldwell wouldn't have touched. Tamara Corbin was no amateur, either, despite her age. Sharp and sharp-tongued, streetwise and nail-tough under her deceptively soft exterior.

Thoughts while he walked, between brief conversations with the inhabitants of Franklin Square. Another indication of life stirring in him again. He hadn't done much thinking the past four months. Mostly just shut his mind down while he went through the zombie motions of daily existence. The way he felt now, with his mind working again, didn't mean rebirth; he wasn't going to wake up whole again some morning. Forming a close bond with Josh wasn't going to happen, either; no illusions about that. But if he could just reach an understanding with his son, then that combined with work should make getting through the days easier, a little more tolerable.

The square was mostly grass and shade trees, a small playground, a fenced-off soccer field in the middle — downscale neighborhood park like any city park that had been taken over by the homeless. Piles of personal belongings were scattered on the grass and footpaths, on a couple of picnic benches; a dozen or so men and women, one of the women young, with a baby slung in a harness over her shoulders, were huddled among the belongings and along the soccer field fence, alone and in pairs and small groups. None of them was a big, dark man in a red and green wool cap. And none would talk to him, once he admitted that he wasn't a cop, unless he offered money first. He doled out spare change and dollar bills, got noninformation in return. Big Dog? Never heard of him. Delia, Mac, Pinkeye? Never heard of them. Spook? Eyes averted, mouths clamped shut. "We don't want nothing to do with murder, man," one of the men said.

Wasted effort until he approached an old

woman sitting alone, cross-legged, on a blanket at the far end of the fence. Next to her was an ancient backpack; in her hands was a container of what smelled like Chinese takeout. She was eating with a plastic spoon, smearing the food into her mouth. Thin, dried out, so wrinkled her blotched face seemed almost mummified, age anywhere from mid-sixties to late-seventies. Bundled up in a worn, patched coat and tattered wool scarf, strands of wispy gray hair showing at the edge of a once-white headpiece like the ones women wore back in the forties. Snood? Something like that.

She fixed him with bright parrotlike eyes when he approached her. He flashed a dollar bill and her eyes got even brighter. "What you want for that, laddie?" She made a cackling noise, showed him a greasy gap-toothed grin. "Delia ain't no woman of easy virtue, you know."

He told her what he wanted. The grin stayed put; so did the brightness in her eyes.

"Big Dog, yeah, I stay clear of that critter," Delia said. "Junkyard dog, that's what he is. Mean. Bite your hand or chew up your leg, you get too close to him when he's had too much wine."

"Where can I find him?"

"Ain't afraid of dogs, laddie? Mean junkyard dogs?"

"No," Runyon said. "Where can I find him?"

"You another cop?"

"Private investigator."

"Like Kojak, huh? No, Kojak was a cop. What you want with that Big Dog?"

"He knew Spook. You know Spook?"

"Sure I knew him. He's dead. Killed."

"Who killed him? Big Dog?"

She cackled again. "Rip your throat out, that junkyard dog, not shoot you with a gun."

"Who do you think did it?"

"Shot Spook? How'd I know? I wasn't there." Delia tapped her temple with a bony forefinger. "Crazy in the head, but he never bothered nobody. Might be it was that fella in the raincoat."

"What fella in the raincoat?"

"Come around here asking about Spook. Looked like a flasher in that raincoat. That's what I thought when he come up, I thought he was gonna flash me. Old fart did that one time, he had a pecker like a pencil." Cackle. "I swear, skinny little thing, just like a pencil. I didn't let him do no writing on me."

"When was this?"

"When was what? When the flasher showed off his little pencil pecker?"

"When the man in the raincoat asked about Spook."

"Sometime. I don't keep track. Few days, a week, who knows?"

"What'd he ask you, exactly?"

"Where he could find a homeless man called Spook."

"He say why he was looking?"

"Nope. Didn't say nothing, just wanted to know where he hung out."

"You tell him where?"

"Nope. Didn't like his looks, didn't like his eyes."

"What was the matter with them?"

"Kind of funny, that's all. All hot and funny, like Big Dog's eyes when he's full up on wine."

"You know if anybody told him where Spook hung out?"

"Don't have no idea. You mean over at that movie place? I like that place. They give you free eats sometimes, fat woman brings 'em out. Not much, not as good as Chinese, that's my favorite, but better'n no eats at all."

"What'd he look like, the man in the raincoat?"

94

" 'Bout your age. Big. Bet *he* didn't have a pencil pecker."

"Big how? Tall, fat, heavyset?"

"Who could tell in a raincoat? Just big, that's all."

"Description?"

"I just told you, didn't I? 'Bout your age and big."

"What color hair?"

"Brown hair. No, black. No, brown. Drizzly that day, that's right, and his hair was wet. Wet and brown and not too much of it. Kinda thin, scalp showing through."

"Beard, mustache?"

"Clean as a whistle, 'cept he had a thing next to his nose."

"A thing?"

"Mole or whatever. Big one."

"Which side, left or right?"

"Uh . . . left. Left side."

"What else was he wearing?"

"Couldn't tell. Raincoat was all buttoned up."

"You're sure it was a raincoat, not an overcoat?"

"What's the difference?"

"Overcoats are bulkier, made of heavy cloth, like mine. Raincoats are lightweight — polyester cotton, microfiber."

"Pretty smart, aren't you?" she said and

cackled. "Wasn't no overcoat. Raincoat. Brown raincoat."

"Old or new? Expensive or inexpensive?"

"Old. Old and wet. Who knows how much it cost? *I* don't." She held out her hand, palm up. "You sure do ask a lot of questions. Ought to be worth more'n just that one dollar, my answers, eh?"

Runyon gave her two singles, watched her make them disappear inside her own threadbare coat. "You tell any of this to the police, Delia?"

"Any of what?"

"About the man in the brown raincoat."

"Nope."

"Why not?"

"They never paid me, that's why not. All cops ever give me is a hard time."

"One more question," Runyon said. "You happen to see what kind of car he was driving? The man in the raincoat."

"Nope. I don't know nothing about cars, don't pay no attention to cars unless I'm crossing the street. This is a dangerous city, you know? They drive their cars like crazy people in this city. Run red lights, don't watch where they're going, one of 'em almost got me in a crosswalk not long ago. Big hurry in their damn fancy cars." Delia tapped her temple again. "Crazy people," she said.

Jack Logan was the only one of the two contact names on duty at the Hall of Justice. He was in his late fifties, salt-and-pepper hair, pepper-and-salt mustache. Quiet, on the reserved side, a little stiff at first. But when Runyon told him who he was working for and sketched out his Seattle background, it produced a warming trend, made Logan almost garrulous.

"Heard a rumor that old Bill was going to retire," he said. "Been meaning to give him a call, but you know how it is — too much work, never enough time. How's he doing? His health, I mean."

"Seems fine."

"Hope so. You can't help wondering when somebody our age decides to pack it in, if maybe they're doing it for health reasons. I always figured an old warhorse like him would stay in harness as long as mind and body permitted."

"Semi-retirement, from what I understand," Runyon said. "Cutting back on his hours, giving up most of the field work."

"Well, that makes more sense. Tired of the grind, I guess. I can sympathize with that." Logan scratched his head, then shook it. "Time catches up with all of us.

Seems to happen all at once, too. One day you're in your prime, the next you're staring geezerhood in the eye and your whole outlook's different, you're not the same man you used to be. In more ways than one."

Runyon said nothing.

"Well, the hell with it. You don't want to listen to that kind of talk and neither do I. So you're Bill's new hire. You'll like working with him. He doesn't always do things by the book, has a tendency to get mixed up in heavy stuff now and then, but he's a good man."

"How about his partner?"

"Partner? Can't mean Eberhardt. He's dead."

"Tamara Corbin."

"He made her a partner? Kid like her? She can't be more than twenty-five."

"Pretty smart for her age, seems like."

"So I hear," Logan said. "I've only met her a couple of times. Cop's daughter, and she's been with Bill four or five years now. Makes sense, if he's cutting back. Times change, all right. People, too."

Again Runyon said nothing.

"So. This Spook business is your first case, you said?"

"That's right. Not a homicide investigation — strictly ID and background search on the victim."

"Let's see what we've got." Logan switched on his computer, punched up the case file. "Bupkus," he said then. "Fingerprint and DNA checks negative, dental check negative, no ID of any kind on the body. Unclaimed John Doe so far."

"Personal items?"

"Not unless you count a pencil stub, two cigarette butts, and a penny."

"Any leads to the perp or to motive?"

"Zero. Forensics didn't find anything at the crime scene or on the vic's clothing. No eyewitnesses, no ear witnesses, nobody on the street knows anything or will admit it if they do. Random assault or personal grudge — most of the homeless homicides come down to one or the other."

"Nothing in the report about a big man with a mole on the left side of his nose, asking questions about Spook a few days before the shooting?"

Logan raised a shaggy eyebrow. "Where'd you get that?"

"An old lady named Delia, in Franklin Square." Runyon summarized the rest of what she'd told him.

"You must be good, to pick that up in a couple of hours."

"Lucky. Right person, right questions."

"Still. Investigating officers should've come up with it. . . ." Logan checked the computer screen. "Oh, yeah, Gunderson." His expression said that Inspector Gunderson was somebody he neither liked nor respected. "Not on duty now, but if you want to talk to him . . ."

"Not much point, is there?"

"Not much," Logan admitted. "I'll pass on the info, for whatever good it'll do. But my guess is this case will wind up in the inactive file — unless you turn up something else in the course of your investigation."

"If I do, it comes straight to you."

"That's what I like to hear from the private sector."

Runyon said, "Be all right if I look at the body?"

"No problem. But it won't do you much good as far as ID goes."

"No?"

"Shot in the back of the head execution style, forty-one caliber weapon, hollow point slug. You know what that means."

"I'd still like a look."

"Suit yourself. I'll call down to the morgue, tell them you're on the way."

A .41 caliber hollow point does a hellish

amount of damage when fired at point-blank range. The upper half of the corpse's face, including both eyes, was gone. The lower half wasn't much better. Bruised and torn flesh from the bullet, decaying teeth, cold-cracked lips, skin lesions, popped blood vessels from alcohol consumption. Age: hard to tell, probably mid-forties, maybe older. Body type: an inch or two under six feet, skinny to the point of emaciation. Identifying characteristics: strawberry birthmark on the upper right arm; thin scar a couple of inches long on the underside of a narrow, pointed chin; long neck with a prominent Adam's apple; knobs on two right finger knuckles that indicated the hand had once been broken.

The most interesting thing was three other scars, old ones, in a place you wouldn't expect to find them — the genital area. The largest measured more than three inches, a curving, jagged line across the abdomen and down alongside the shriveled scrotum. The other two were on the penis itself, one across the top, one on the left side, that had deformed its shape. As if he'd been slashed down there with some kind of sharp instrument.

The morgue attendant, standing to one side of the sliding refrigerator drawer, saw where Runyon was looking under the lifted sheet. He said, "Looks like somebody tried to castrate him once."

"Or he tried to do it himself."

"Jesus, why would a guy want to cut off his own dick?"

"This one had mental problems."

"His mental problems didn't shoot his face off," the attendant said. "You through here?"

"I'm through."

The attendant sheeted the body again, slid the drawer shut. "Poor bugger," he said. "Some life he must've had. At least now he don't have to eat any more of the sandwich."

"What sandwich is that?"

"Shit sandwich. Friend of mine says that's what life is for most people — a shit sandwich, and every day we take another bite."

"A philosopher, your friend."

"Yeah. You agree with him?"

"He won't get any argument from me."

7

Jake Runyon

He spent the rest of the afternoon cruising the area within a ten-block radius of Visuals, Inc. No sign of Big Dog in Franklin Square or on the streets or in the soup kitchen or homeless shelter or among the handful of wary occupants of a cluttered, junk-infested encampment under the freeway interchange. A few of the street people he talked to owned up to knowing who Big Dog was, but none could or would say where he hung out. Most refused to say anything, even when money was offered. Even the soup kitchen and shelter volunteers were reluctant to speak freely. Fear seemed to be the motivating factor, not of Runyon or what he represented, but of Big Dog and of becoming involved in a homicide.

Runyon didn't blame them. The thick shit sandwich out here was hard enough to swallow without adding dead meat and hair from a junkyard dog to the loaf.

At dusk he called it quits for the day. The wind had sharpened, turned gusty, and the smell of rain was in the air. Raw night ahead. Most of the homeless were already forted up; the soup kitchen had long lines and the shelter had been nearly full at four o'clock. Trouble, not answers, was what you invited by prowling unfamiliar territory on a cold, wet winter night.

No food since a skimpy breakfast and he was hungry. He'd gone days without eating after Colleen died, but once he was away from Seattle his appetite had gradually returned. Two meals a day now, and starting to put back some of the weight he'd lost. He stopped at a Chinese restaurant on his way across Twin peaks, packed in a three-course meal. Egg rolls, mooshu pork, crispy Peking chicken — Colleen's favorites. They'd eaten Chinese two or three times a week before she got sick, usually in the same little hole-in-the-wall off Pioneer Square. He'd continued the ritual after he moved down here, in honor of her and what they'd shared. Another way of keeping her memory close.

His apartment was on Ortega, a few blocks off 19th Avenue, on the city's west side. Four rooms, furnished, on the third floor of an old, anonymous stucco building. When the real estate agent first showed him the place, he'd automatically cataloged each room and its contents down to the last detail. Now that he'd lived there for more than a month, he'd've been hard-pressed when away to say what color the living room walls were or whether or not there was a carpet in the bedroom. Familiarity made the details nonessential. That was the way his mind worked in professional circumstances: Particulars noted, retained for as long as necessary, then filed for future reference or erased completely from his memory banks, depending on their relative importance to the business at hand.

Cold night, cold apartment. He turned on the heat, went into the kitchen to brew himself a cup of tea. Colleen's drink, now his. The fifth of Wild Turkey was stored in the same cupboard with the package of darjeeling, still almost half full. Emergency rations. Colleen's phrase: "We ought to keep emergency rations on hand, just in case we suddenly have something to celebrate." Or something to mourn. They'd gotten into the emergency rations just twice, the first time when he was promoted from patrolman to detective, the second when one of her sculptures sold for $300 at a crafts fair. He'd gotten into the whiskey just once on his own, the night she died. Booze was a crutch. He didn't need a crutch, unless you counted work as one. The things he needed he could never have — a time machine and a cure for ovarian cancer. But he'd brought the bottle along anyway. Not because he might need it again; because it was something else they'd shared.

He took his tea into the living room, flipped on the TV. Five minutes of the seven o'clock news was all he could take. He shut the set off, sat there in the silence for a time, and then without thinking about it he got up and went to the phone. No need to look up the number. He'd dialed it often enough in the past few weeks.

And listened often enough to the same silly recorded message. "Hello. This is the disembodied voice of Joshua Fleming. Leave your name and number and my real self will return your call as soon as it materializes."

Screening his calls all the time now, probably. The first call he'd answered, but as soon as Runyon said, "Josh, this is your father," he'd broken the connection. Answering machine every call since. And still not one returned.

The beep sounded in his ear. He said, "It's me again, son. I don't enjoy pestering you, no matter what you might think, but I'm not giving up until we talk at least once. Pick up if you're there."

Silence.

All right. He recited his number again, started to lower the receiver, then brought it back up. "Please," he said. "It's almost Christmas."

Too quiet in the apartment. He put the television back on for noise, surfed up an old movie — *Casablanca*, one of Colleen's favorites — and sat staring at it without comprehending much of what was going on. His mind was on Joshua.

He'd come close to bracing him two weeks ago, when he'd gone down to Embarcadero Center to the firm of financial planners where Josh worked as a trainee. No good reason for going except to see what the place was like, maybe get a look at him from a distance. He'd got the look, all right, from a dozen feet away in the building lobby, but before he could make up his mind whether to speak to him, Josh had faded into the crowd. Just as well. Catching him off guard like that would've been a mistake; probably alienated him even more.

No longer a kid now, his son. Twenty-two and a man. Tallish, handsome in a pretty-boy way, with Andrea's blond hair and blue eyes and narrow mouth. Otherwise, a stranger. Nothing of his father in appearance or mannerisms or the way he moved, and damn little, if any, of his mental or psychological makeup. If even a hint of Jake Runyon had manifested itself in Joshua in his early years, Andrea would have made sure to leech it out of him. Hell hath no fury. Her son, her image, her hate-child to the bitter end.

He watched the movie for a while, still without internalizing much of it except for the scene in Rick's Café when the French patriots begin singing "La Marseillaise" to drown out the Nazis' drunken rendition of "Deutschland über Alles." Stirring stuff that had made Colleen cry every time. Lots of things made her cry. What was that phrase from one of the other old movies she'd liked, the one set in Japan with Glenn Ford? Cry for happy, that was it. She'd cried at the drop of a hat, but mostly it had been crying for happy. It wasn't until the goddamn cancer that she'd cried for sad, cried for scared, cried for hurt, and that he'd started crying with her.

The phone rang.

Runyon's first thought was telemarketer. He'd had maybe half a dozen incoming calls since he'd lived here, and all but two — the two from his new employer — had been telemarketers. Invasion of privacy at the best of times, and this wasn't the best of times. He went over and answered it, snapping his "Hello," ready to snap harder once the pitch began.

The voice on the other end said formally, grudgingly, "This is Joshua Fleming."

For a few seconds the words ground his mental gears, stalled his thoughts. "Well," he said, and it sounded stupid. He cleared his throat and said, "Thanks for getting in touch." And that sounded stupid, too.

"I'm tired of all the messages on my answering machine." Cold and flat and tight with contained anger. Like Andrea's voice the few times he'd tried to talk to her after the separation and divorce. The only difference was that hers had dripped loathing like acid. "Why did you have to move down here? Why can't you just leave me alone?"

"I had nowhere else to go," Runyon said.

"You could have stayed in Seattle."

"No, I couldn't. Not after . . . well, you know about my wife."

"Yeah, I know." That was all — no expression of sympathy. "It doesn't change anything."

"I think it does. You're all I have left now."

"Then you don't have anything left now."

"You're my son, Josh."

"My name is Joshua, not Josh."

"All right. My son Joshua."

"Like hell I'm your son. I stopped being your son the day you left my mother and me twenty years ago."

"I've tried to make up for that. The whole time you were growing up, I tried. Your mother —"

"You put her through hell, you have no idea how much she suffered."

"It wasn't just me who made her suffer."

"You didn't know her. You never did."

"Is that what she told you?"

"You don't know me, either. Anything about me."

"I want to know you."

"Well, I don't want to know you."

"We need to talk, Joshua."

"Why? There's nothing you can say that I want to hear."

110

"I'm going to say it anyway, sooner or later."

"Fine, then go ahead, say it."

"Not on the phone. Face to face, man to man."

"No."

"In a public place, if you want it that way. Lunch, dinner, drinks."

"I don't drink."

Good, Runyon thought, that's one good thing you learned growing up with her. "One meeting, one conversation. That's all I'm asking."

"I don't believe you."

"I'm not a liar, son. Whatever else you think of me, believe that. I never lied to your mother. I'll never lie to you."

"So you say. Why should I give you the opportunity?"

"Why not? What can one meeting hurt? If you still want nothing to do with me afterward, okay, I won't bother you anymore."

Circuit hum. Then, "Does that include leaving San Francisco?"

"I have a job here now. City's big enough for both of us, isn't it?"

"It's *my* city, my mother's city, not yours."

"I meant what I said. One meeting, straight talk, and after that the ball's in your court."

". . . You just won't give up, will you?"

"Not before we talk."

More humming silence. Somebody, not Joshua, said something in the background in a low whisper.

"Who was that?"

"My roommate. He thinks I should go ahead, get it over with."

"What do you say?"

"I say you're spoiling my holidays."

"Not my intention. Peace for both of us, that's all I'm after."

"Man, that's really profound. You're a profound guy, aren't you?"

"When can we meet? You name the time and place."

No answer.

"Any day, anywhere you say."

"Oh, Christ," Joshua said. Then, as if he were hurling the words, "All right. All right, I'll let you know, I'll leave a message on *your* machine this time," and the receiver went down hard on the other end.

Runyon returned to the couch. *Casablanca* was over; some other movie had started. He shut off the TV. Then he switched off the lamp and sat in the dark, alternately thinking and not thinking, waiting for it to be time for bed and sleep.

112

8

Monday was one of those dark, dreary December days — cold, light rain, low-hanging clouds. My mood was pretty upbeat in spite of the weather, but not Tamara's; she blew in like a raincloud, wet and sullen. Uncommunicative, too. She growled unintelligibly at my "Good morning," grumbled likewise at my offer of a cup of coffee, threw her coat at the rack — it slid off the hook to puddle on the floor, where she left it — and stomped to her desk. On went her computer; she sat there glowering at it.

"Okay," I said, "what'd you do with her?"

Mutter that sounded like "Who?"

"New Tamara, the pleasant one. I could swear I'm looking at Old Tamara, the gloomy, irascible brat."

Another mutter, this one with a four-letter word in it.

"Uh-huh," I said. "Definitely Old Tamara. I never did like her much."

Silence.

I made a couple more futile efforts to jolly her out of her mood. Then I went and refilled my cup at the hotplate as an excuse to take a closer look at her. Puffy cheeks, baggage under her eyes, the whites shot through with red veins. Not New Tamara, not Old Tamara — an alarmingly different Tamara.

"You want to talk about it?" I said, serious now.

"No."

"Something happen over the weekend? Looks like you haven't had much sleep."

"I'm okay," she lied. "Don't worry your head about me."

"Come on, Ms. Corbin. I'm a detective, I can deduce the difference between okay and not okay."

Mutter.

"I didn't get that."

"Said I don't want to talk about him."

"Who?"

Silence.

"Tamara, who is it you don't want to talk about?"

She made eye contact for the first time. Her expression was more than just haggard; it was etched with pain, the mental kind. "It's all over," she said. "Finished, kaput."

"What is? You don't mean you and Horace?"

"Man wants me to marry him."

"He what?"

"Marry his sorry ass. I moved out on Saturday."

"I don't get that. Moved out?"

"Staying with Claudia till I can find someplace else," she said, and pulled a face. "Vonda doesn't have a spare room, Lucille's mother's living with her now, wasn't anybody else."

I stared at her. Claudia was her older sister, Vonda and Lucille were two of her girlfriends. That much made sense, but the rest of it . . . "You moved out on Horace because he asked you to marry him?"

"No way I'm going to Philadelphia with him."

". . . Where did Philadelphia come from?"

"His big dream. Seat with a symphony orchestra."

"In Philadelphia? Good for him, but —"

"Audition last Friday, now he's got his big chance."

"So it's definite?"

"Definite enough. Has to practice with the orchestra first, but they wouldn't be paying his way if he wasn't gonna get the

115

gig. Besides, he's a fine cellist. Gonna get better, too, maybe in Yo-Yo Ma's class someday, wouldn't surprise me."

"Well, then, you can't blame him for —"

"I don't blame him. Go to Philly, play his cello, have his dream, have a nice life."

"Are you saying he gave you some kind of ultimatum? Marry him and move back east, or it's all over between you?"

"No. But he *expected* it, you know what I'm saying?"

Jake Runyon walked in just then and put an end to this confusing exchange. Tamara glowered at him and began to pound her computer keyboard. He glanced at me, nodded when I made a go-easy gesture behind Tamara's back. Horace situation on hold.

I asked Runyon how things had gone on Saturday afternoon. He said, "Turned up a few things, nothing definite," and gave me a terse rundown.

"Those genital scars might be an angle if we can get a general fix on where Spook came from," I said. "Can't be many near-castration cases on record."

Tamara had been listening. She muttered, "Be one in San Francisco if that man don't keep his distance."

When a woman is in a mood like hers, all

116

primed and loaded and ready to go off, the smartest thing a man can do is to ignore her. Runyon knew it, too. He said to me, "Pretty severe wounds, self-inflicted or not. Professionally treated, from the look of the scars. Bound to be hospital records somewhere."

"You think there might be a connection to those ghosts of his?"

"Could be. The guy with the mole I can't figure yet."

"Odds are he's the shooter."

"Or a scout for the shooter. Linked somehow, anyway."

"Probably."

"Question is, why track down and blow away a disturbed homeless man? Homeless and harmless, by all accounts."

"Motive might be tied up in who Spook was, his background."

"Maybe. You have anything else for me today?"

"I don't think so. Tamara?"

"Nothing pressing except the job for McCone Investigations."

"Almost finished with that. My baby, anyway."

Runyon said, "Then I'd like to work the streets again, try to get leads on the guy with the mole and this Big Dog character."

"Okay. Go ahead."

"Just remember to check in," Tamara said, "you find something or not."

"I won't forget."

I said, "One thing before you go, Jake. You own a firearm?"

"Three-five-seven Magnum."

"You'll need to get it registered in California. Bonding company requirement."

"Already taken care of. Soon as I had a permanent address."

"Premises?"

"And carry, both."

I raised an eyebrow. "You must've pulled a string somewhere to get a carry permit without bonafide employment."

"A couple of strings," Runyon said. "All in who you know."

"Ain't that the truth."

When he was gone, I said to Tamara, "About you and Horace —"

That was far as I got. She swung around on me, scowling and sparking. "I don't want to talk about him anymore. That's all I been doing since Friday night, talking to or about that man."

"I'm sorry, I know it must be hard for you."

"Just don't be telling me we can work something out. He keeps saying it, Claudia keeps saying it, I don't want to hear it out anybody else's mouth."

"Okay. No questions, no comments, no advice. Peace and quiet in the workplace."

That bought me one of her slitty-eyed looks. "You sure you a man, all nice and reasonable like that?"

"Last time I looked."

"Hah. Now that's typical, comes down to that every time."

"What does?"

"How a man thinks. Ask him if he's sure he's a man, right away he says 'Last time I looked.' Dude that used to draw 'Bloom County,' he had it right on."

" 'Bloom County'?"

"One strip, this feminist tells Opus and Bill the Cat to take another look at the one thing gives meaning to their meaningless lives, and what do they do?"

I had no idea who Opus or Bill the Cat were. "I don't know, what?"

"Drag open their shorts and stare at their dicks. Never catch a woman saying 'Last time I looked' and opening her panty hose and staring at her —"

"Never mind! Let's just drop the subject, shall we?"

"Men," she muttered, and went back to abusing her keyboard.

I had two cases working. The least important was an employee investigation for one of the city's small engineering firms; the employee was in a position of some trust, and the head of the firm had cause to suspect that the trust had been violated — that the employee might be passing bid specs to a rival company. The priority case was the subcontract for McCone Investigations.

Sharon McCone was an old friend, and in small ways something of a protégé. Her agency down on the bayfront had prospered in recent years, to the point where she now had a staff of six and a caseload that many times larger than the one Tamara and I carried. By dint of several high-profile cases, she'd developed a reputation for results that now and then brought her plum jobs. The most recent was a politically and media sensitive investigation of the city's building-inspection department. It had started out as a relatively simple probe into whether or not a senior official, one Joseph Patterson, was taking kickbacks in exchange for speeding up the permit process, but it had blossomed into a revelation of corruption in other arms of city government. The group that had hired her, headed by the deputy mayor, was clamoring for fast action, and in order to satisfy them McCone and her overworked staff needed help with certain aspects of the investigation. Occasionally in such situations she subcontracted work to other operatives like Tamara and me.

Our part of the inquiry had been fairly extensive, if routine, and some of the information I'd dug up had turned out to be vital — McCone's word when I passed it on to her. The entire case was close to the finish now. A few more chunks of hard evidence, and she'd turn over enough ammunition to the deputy mayor and the D.A. to prosecute Patterson and two of his cronies and to remove a few others from their entrenchment in the city pork barrel.

But the last chunk from us would have to wait a while longer. The two calls I made produced zero results, both sources being unavailable until later in the day. There wasn't much else I could do until I talked to them.

Dead silence in the office now. Tamara was sitting zombielike, staring off into space. Hurting and angry and full of gloom; I could almost see the dark cloud hanging above her head, like the character in Li'l Abner. As sorry as I felt for her, her bleak mood was having an effect on me. I decided I needed an airing. Work on the engineering employee job could wait until later, and it was getting on toward lunch time and I was hungry. Imminent semiretirement had done wonders for my appetite. If I didn't watch out, it would eventually do greater wonders for my waistline.

I told Tamara where I was going, that I'd be back around one. Her response was a grunt. Who says it's so great to be young? I thought, and beat it out of there before youth took another bite out of my Monday.

9

Tamara

She spent most of the morning on a search for an insurance company client — hospital medical records that were supposed to be private. Hah. Wasn't much of anything that was private these days. Small hospital up in southern Oregon, no cooperation through regular channels, so she'd hacked into their files. On the side of the angels here, right? Subject claimed he'd developed severe stress problems on his job that led to a mild stroke, wanted his firm's insurance company to pay all medical expenses and provide a disability package. Said he'd never been treated for high blood pressure or any other stress-related illness. Flat-out lie. Hospital records said he'd been in there twice, once in the emergency room after passing out on the street, diagnosis both times of dangerously high blood pressure exacerbated by alcohol abuse. Given prescriptions for blood thinners and strongly advised to quit drinking. (Didn't take the advice or the blood thinners; other searches proved that.) Both parents confirmed alcoholics, father also had high blood pressure and died of a stroke. Oh, yeah, this sorry-ass dude was toast in more ways than one.

She highlighted the records, tapped the print key. Feeling a little better now, with nobody around to hassle her. Just her and Mac doing their thing to keep her mind off all the crap in her life —

The door opened and somebody came in.

She looked up. Oh, Lord, she thought.

He came in slow and easy, the way he always entered a room, kind of gliding like a big old cat. Raindrops glistened on his coat and that out-of-shape gray hat with the moldy feather in the band. She hated that hat; everybody hated that hat except him. His lucky Fedora, he called it. Lucky it didn't have a mess of lice crawling around inside it.

"Morning, sweetness," he said.

That damn nickname. Made her sound like a female Walter Payton. Sometimes she didn't mind it; other times, when she was feeling bad like now, it set her teeth on edge. Him and his pro football. Biggest disappointment of his life was hurting his knee his senior year at San Jose State and never getting a tryout at defensive back with one of the pro teams.

She said, trying to keep the annoyance out of her voice, "What're you doing here, Pop?"

"Had to come to the city on police business. So I thought I'd stop by, see how you're doing."

Yeah, sure. "Doing fine," she said.

"That's not what I hear."

"Claudia called you, right? Damn that girl! I told her —"

"Don't curse your sister. I haven't talked to her in a week."

"Well, then, how —"

"Horace. Last night."

"*He* called you? What, so you'd try to talk me around to his side?"

"He loves you, Tamara."

"I know it. Doesn't change anything."

Pop took off his hat, ran a hand over his knobby head. Hairline receded more every time she saw him, seemed like; bald about halfway back now. Maybe that was why he wore that hat all the time. The long bushy mustache, too — a kind of compensation. Always was vain about his looks.

He'd been here before, once, to look the place over and meet the boss man. Made up an excuse for showing up that time, too; couldn't just come out and admit he was checking up. But now he was looking around like it was his first visit.

"This office is pretty low-end," he said. "Fits the neighborhood."

"Rent's cheap."

"Still. Might be a good idea to upgrade your image."

"Talk to the boss man about it, not me."

"He's not the boss man anymore, is he? Equal partners?"

"Not until next month. Still the boss man, anyway. I'll be the boss *woman*."

"So talk to him about new office space."

"He's the one built the agency, holds it together. He wants us to stay here, we'll stay here. Knamean?"

"Don't use that tone with me, girl."

"What tone?"

"Little kid snotty. You know I don't like it."

"Just telling it like it is, Pop."

"Like you told Horace how it is?"

She ground molars, swallowed a breath before she said, "Don't be ragging on me, okay?"

"You going to sit down with the man?"

"Already sat down with him. It's all talked out."

"He doesn't think so."

"Not giving up my career for him."

"Some career for a young African American woman."

"Following in your footsteps."

"I'm a police officer, not a private detective. I never wanted you girls involved in any kind of law enforcement."

"And we done defied you. Claudia got her law degree and went to work for the D.A. instead of going into private practice and I turned into a private eye. Big disappointment for you and Ma."

"For God's sake, we're not disappointed. We're proud of you both. I'm only saying —"

"Please, Pop. I don't want to hear anymore about my career or Horace and me. Decision's mine, nobody else's."

"You don't have to move to Philadelphia to make your relationship work."

"Long distance romance? That's honky movie stuff, not real life."

"Watch your mouth. We taught you better than that."

"I mean it," she said. "I'm looking to build my life right here. What's wrong with that?"

"Building it alone, that's what's wrong with it."

"Marriage, kids? Been getting along fine without, so far."

"You wouldn't be here if your mother and me thought that way."

That old song. She said, "It's not for everybody, you know that."

He went over and laid a hip on the corner of Bill's cluttered desk. Out came one of his sticks of spearmint gum. Always chewing that stuff since he quit smoking. "We had hopes you'd come around," he said. "You and Horace make a handsome couple."

"Bull, Pop. You couldn't stand him when I first brought him home."

"Wrong first impression," he admitted. "What kind of man wants to play a cello for a living? But I came around. He's strong, smart, and he's been good to you. Seemed right that you'd get married eventually."

"No way," Tamara said. Lie or truth? She didn't know. If Horace *had* asked her under the right circumstances . . . Too late now anyway.

"You keep saying that. How about if the three of us sit down, I help you try to come to an understanding?"

"Dag, that's a fine idea. Me and Horace, and Sergeant Dennis Corbin, Redwood City PD, handling the interrogation.

That'd sure solve everything."

"Snotty again. Knock it off!"

"I will, if you'll please just stay out of my business."

"You are my business, girl. You and Claudia. Two healthy daughters, raised the best we knew how, and you —"

The telephone cut him off. Tamara swooped down on it. Contact returning one of the boss man's calls on the job for McCone Investigations. She took down his information, writing it in longhand rather than on the Mac to prolong the conversation. When she finally hung up, Pop was on his feet again — giving her that look of his, half glum and half evil-eye, like when she was a kid and she'd done something to piss him off.

"Almost noon," he said. "I'll buy you lunch."

"Can't today. Too much work."

"You have to eat."

"Catch a sandwich later."

He hesitated, sighed, started toward the door, stopped again. "You can't just leave it like this with Horace," he said.

"So long, Pop. Thanks for coming by."

The look for a few more seconds. Then he slapped that sorry old hat back on his head, said, "We'll talk again soon," and went on out before she could say anything else.

Men. Fathers. Lord have mercy.

Phone rang again. Damn phone. She managed not to growl when she picked up.

Jake Runyon. He said, "I'm at Visuals, Inc. Found something that might be useful, might not. Thought you'd want to know in any case."

"Go ahead."

"Came from one of the equipment handlers, Pete Snyder. He was on vacation last week, didn't know Spook was dead until this morning. He told me a woman from the Department of Human Services mentioned Spook a few days before the shooting."

"Social worker?"

"Homeless caseworker. But Spook wasn't one of hers."

"What was her interest in him then?"

"No interest. She took a call about him."

Tamara's nerves twanged again. "Don't drag it out, man, get to the point."

"The point," Runyon said evenly, "is that the social worker took a call about Spook at her office. Somebody wanted to know where to find him."

"Who?"

"She didn't give Snyder a name."

130

"Caller say why he was looking for Spook?"

"If he did, she didn't pass it on."

"Well, what did she pass on?"

"Just what I told you."

"Then why'd she come around to talk to him about it?"

"Look, Tamara . . . Ms. Corbin . . . I don't mind being growled at when I've done something to warrant it, but this isn't one of those times. I'm just doing my job here. Suppose we keep things on a professional level until my ass deserves chewing on?"

She bristled and framed a comeback, but the bristle went and the comeback didn't get said. Man was right. She didn't have any reason to rag on him; she was venting on Horace, on men in general. Get a grip, girl.

"Sorry," she said. "I'm usually not a bitch-slapper — just a bad time for me right now. Personal stuff."

"Okay. I've been there."

Yeah, he had. Still was. Place he was in right now was a lot worse than the one she was in. "The social worker . . . why'd she go talk to Snyder about Spook?"

"She didn't," Runyon said. "He eats lunch in the same place every day, a res-

131

taurant over on Potrero. She goes there sometimes when she's in the neighborhood. They were both there the day after she got the call, that's when she mentioned it to Snyder."

"Few days before the shooting, you said?"

"Friday before last."

"What's the social worker's name?"

"Evelyn something. Snyder doesn't know her last name. Young, Japanese. A stone fox, he says."

"Uh-huh. Meaning he hit on her and she blew him off."

"You want me to follow up or keep on Big Dog?"

"Big Dog," she said.

"I'll be in touch."

Homeless caseworker, Japanese, young, and a fox — shouldn't be too hard to track down. Agency didn't have any contacts in the Department of Human Services, and people in city office jobs could be uncooperative with strangers on the phone. Might as well give it a try, though, see what shook out. She had her hand on the receiver when the bell jangled again, making her jump. Damn phone!

Boss man, this time. "Just checking in," he said. "You going out for lunch or you want me to bring you something?"

"Not hungry," Tamara said. She passed along the message on the Patterson case, then Runyon's info on the social worker.

"You contact Human Services yet?"

"Just about to."

"I'm down near City Hall," he said. "I'll stop over there, see if I can locate the woman. City workers tend to be more cooperative in person."

"Fact. Just now thinking the same thing."

"Great minds."

"Yeah," she said.

Only problem with his was, it was inside a man's head.

10

It took me all of thirty seconds at Human Services to find out the social worker's full name: Evelyn Sukimoto. But it was a good three hours before I could get an audience with her.

She was out of the office, the young starchy type I spoke to said, and wouldn't be back until mid-afternoon. Yes, she had a cell phone, but he couldn't give me the number without her permission. No, he couldn't tell me where she was now.

I said, "Mid-afternoon. That mean three o'clock?"

He offered up one of those looks young people reserve for those of us past the age of forty, the kind that equates age with creeping senility. "Ms. Sukimoto," he said firmly, "will be back at her desk mid-afternoon."

Young, frozen-faced, on the supercilious side, and knew just how to make an imprecise statement sound precise and authoritative. A perfect candidate for the mayor's public relations team. Hizzoner was going to need more spin doctors once the Patterson scandal broke. I considered telling Frozen Face he ought to apply, but suppose he took me seriously and went ahead and did it? Sobering thought. I settled for a toothy grin and a broad wink, and left him sitting there to puzzle that one out.

Rather than return to the office, I checked in with Tamara again on the car phone. I'd had enough today, up close and personal, of her blue funk. Two more messages, which she delivered in a terse growl. Any further word from Jake Runyon? No. Anything to discuss? No.

One of the messages had to do with the investigation for the engineering firm; I returned that call first, but the guy was away from his desk. Telephone tag. The other message was from Ted Smalley, the office manager at McCone Investigations. I had no trouble getting him on the line.

"Almost done here, Ted. One more thing to verify and I'll have everything fully documented."

"How soon, do you think?"

"Shouldn't be long. Tomorrow, Wednesday at the latest."

"Can you get the complete file to us by midday Thursday? Sharon wants everything wrapped up by close of business Friday so we can all enjoy the party. She has a meeting scheduled with the deputy mayor and the D.A. on Monday morning."

"I don't see any problem. They're not fixing to break the story before Christmas, are they?"

"No, not until after the holidays," Ted said. "But the D.A. is eager to start preparing his indictments. Naturally. He has his eye on the state attorney general's seat."

"Uh-huh. So I've heard."

"The party is the other reason I called — to make sure you and Kerry will be attending. Tamara, too, of course."

"Party?"

"The pier's Season of Sharing party. I mentioned it to you last week."

"Oh, right. Right."

"You will be coming?"

"It's on the calendar," I said without enthusiasm.

"Sharon will be very disappointed if you're a no-show."

"We'll be there, Ted. But I wouldn't count on Tamara."

"Oh? Why not?"

"Personal problems. Not too serious." I hope, I added silently. "What time again? Seven?"

"Six. Six to nine. Come early."

"I'm looking forward to it," I lied.

The fact is, I don't much enjoy parties of any kind. Large gatherings, no matter how festive or charitable, make me feel claustrophobic; I don't mix well, I'm no good at small talk, even with people I know, and my mind inevitably goes blank and shrivels up like a moldy nut in a shell. Kerry keeps trying to socialize me and it keeps not working. The quiet of home and hearth is what I prefer, the more so during the Christmas season. The one other large holiday party I'd attended, at her insistence — the infamous Gala Family Christmas Charity Benefit years ago — had been an unmitigated disaster for several reasons, not the least of which was my having allowed myself to be stuffed into a Santa Claus suit and little kiddies to dent my knees while they shared their innermost toy lusts.

The Season of Sharing affair wouldn't be that bad. It too was an annual charity benefit, but on a much smaller scale, put on by McCone Investigations and the other businesses at Pier 24-½. I'd been to a couple of them — Sharon is one of the last persons I would ever willingly offend — and I had survived. I'd survive this one, too, if I approached it in the right spirit.

And the right spirit started with not worrying about it days in advance. What I needed right now was a way to pass the time until mid-afternoon. The only one with any appeal had nothing to do with business. Well, so what? Might as well start getting rid of the workaholic mindset a couple of weeks ahead of schedule.

I drove up to Pacific Heights, lucked into a parking space a block from the building that houses my flat. My soon-to-be-former flat. The decision to semiretire had come with a corollary: get rid of unnecessary possessions and consolidate my life. I'd had the rent-controlled flat almost as long as I'd been a freelance investigator, and for a time after Kerry and I were married I'd split my time between it and her Diamond Heights condo — an unconventional arrangement that had worked pretty well, giving both of us the space and privacy we needed after years of living alone. But gradually I'd found myself spending more and more time at the condo; it was home now, and had been even before Emily came into our lives. Over the past year I'd slept a total of two nights at the flat, both for business-related reasons. The place no longer felt the same to me. It was as if, walking in, I was entering a series of rooms that were only distantly familiar, like a house or apartment where you lived many years ago; as if I'd already moved out. A little more than two weeks, and it would cease to be mine. New year, new lease for somebody else. I wondered if I'd miss it any after I turned over the keys. Maybe a little, but not much.

There were only a few things left here that I wanted to keep. One piece of furniture, an antique secretary desk. Some personal stuff. And the bulk of my collection of 6,000 pulp magazines. There was room at the condo for all of these, though we'd need to do some rearranging and buy several new bookcases.

Cartons of pulps that I'd already packed were piled in the living room; only about two thousand were left on shelves. Several more cartons containing my long run of *Black Mask* and other valuable titles I'd already transported to the condo. I took off my coat and set to work filling the few remaining empty boxes, making another mental note to round up additional empties before my next visit. Maybe this time, with four or five such notes stored, I would remember to do it.

Pulp-paper magazines, with their gaudy covers and brittle, untrimmed edges and melodramatic stories of a vanished era, were a pleasure to handle. Even tucked into protective Mylar bags, their faintly musty odor permeated a room in a heady sort of way. I'd started collecting them in my late teens, and at one time I'd been an active, even aggressive buyer, poring over sales catalogs and haunting used bookshops and flea markets in my spare time. But then I'd met Kerry, and there'd been other changes good and bad, capped by Emily's arrival, and my interest in pulps had declined to the point where I seldom even looked at them anymore.

Now, though, with more free time in the offing, my enthusiasm had rekindled. I'd started unbagging and reading stories at random, here and at the condo. I'd dug out my old want list of missing issues of *Black Mask*, *Dime Detective*, and half a dozen other titles and given it to Ted Smalley's significant other, Neal Osborn, who was an antiquarian bookseller with worldwide contacts. Once I had the entire collection moved and reshelved, I would catalog it and then begin upgrading the tattier issues.

The prospect was energizing. Who said work was the be-all and end-all of a man's existence? Who said retirement was just a period of limbo between living and dying? Me, once, but not anymore.

I packed up six cartons and hauled them out to the car. Two at a time, just to prove that I could do it without working up much of a sweat.

Mid-afternoon did not mean three o'clock, after all, not in the Department of Human Services. Evelyn Sukimoto wasn't there when I walked in at five minutes before three. She wasn't there at three-fifteen, or at three-thirty. At twenty to four I caught the smarmy young guy giving me a satisfied little grin, as if he enjoyed watching me sit and wait. He'd make a perfect spin doctor, all right. Help cover backsides, help screw the citizens who didn't contribute campaign funds and couldn't be bought. Up the machine! Politics for politicians! Don't legislate, obfuscate and manipulate!

People came in, people went out. Staff, mostly, a good ethnic mix of African Americans, Latinos, Asians, and Caucasians. The younger ones wore determined, upbeat expressions, moved with a certain brisk purpose; the older ones seemed tired and stoic, their movements almost lethargic. No surprise there. Urban social work is a young person's game. The players under thirty believe they can make a difference, and work hard at the job. The veterans have had too many daily encounters with grinding poverty, alcoholism, drug abuse, spousal abuse, street abuse, plus all the myriad forms of political b.s., to retain an outward show of optimism. Some had turned bitter, cynical. Even the ones who remained idealists at heart had a defeated, worn-out demeanor, like structurally sound buildings with weathered, graffiti-scarred facades.

Evelyn Sukimoto was one of the young, determined variety. She showed up finally at two minutes past four, fast-stepping as if she couldn't wait to get to her desk. She was about twenty-five, slender, nice features; silky, glistening black hair hung almost to her waist. Frozen Face glanced up at her as she approached his desk, then quickly avoided eye contact by peering again at his computer screen. Right in character: He wasn't going to tell her she had a visitor. But I was already on my feet, and I got to her before she could pass through to the inner sanctum.

"Ms. Sukimoto?"

She didn't know me and I didn't look homeless, but she offered up a nice little smile anyway. "Yes?"

I said I'd been waiting to talk to her and could she give me ten minutes or so of her time? "It's about the homeless man who was murdered last week. Spook."

She lost the smile. "Are you with the police?"

"Private investigator." I proved it to her with my license photostat, told her what we'd been retained to do.

"Well . . . all right, come with me."

We went through the door, then through a maze of cubicles to one with her name on a little plate next to its doorless entrance. Desk, desk chair, straight-backed chair, and not much else. We both sat down.

"I don't know how I can help you," she said. "Spook wasn't one of my clients; I hardly knew him. Why did you come to me?"

I relayed what Jake Runyon had told Tamara. The smile came back, sliced wry this time, when she heard Pete Snyder's name.

"Uh-huh," she said. "Pete the Stud."

"Stud?"

"He thinks so, anyway. Hits on me every time he sees me."

"Sounds like you don't much like him."

"What's to like? He's married, for one thing. Even if he wasn't, I wouldn't have anything to do with him."

"Too pushy?"

"Too white. I don't date white guys."

I couldn't think of anything to say to that.

"I was married to one for ten months. That's why."

Or to that.

"Not that I'm bitter or anything," Ms. Sukimoto lied. "It's just that . . . well, he was such a shit. My ex, I mean. And you know the old expression. Once burned, twice shy."

I made a polite noise this time. Intended it to be polite, at least. It came out sounding like a dyspeptic grunt.

"Anyway, like I said, I hardly knew that poor man. Murdered . . . my God, of all people. I still have trouble believing it. But I don't know a thing about him or why he was killed."

"You told Snyder you'd had an inquiry about Spook. A caller who wanted to know where to find him."

"Well, *I* didn't have an inquiry. I mean,

the man on the phone didn't ask for me, specifically."

"Who did he ask for?"

"Spook's caseworker. Janet Coolibra."

"By name?"

"No, I don't think so. The call was referred to Janet's number. She had to go out for a few minutes and she was expecting another call, so she asked me to pick up for her. That's how I happened to talk to the man."

"Did he identify himself?"

"No. All he said was that he was trying to locate a homeless man named Spook."

"You ask him why?"

"He said Spook might be somebody he knew once. And if so, maybe he could help him get off the streets."

"And you told him about Visuals, Inc.?"

"I didn't know about Visuals, Inc. then. Even if I had known, I wouldn't have given out the information to a stranger over the phone."

"Did you give him Janet's name?"

"Yes. He said he'd contact her."

"Did he, do you know?"

"He didn't. She never heard from him."

"How did he sound to you? Young, old?"

"Not young."

"How old, would you say?"

"Well . . . not ancient, but . . . you know, an older man."

That statement was accompanied by a sidewise flick of her gaze, as if she were thinking, *You know, somebody your age.* Youth is a wonderful thing — if you happen to be looking at the world through young eyes.

I asked, "How would you characterize his tone?"

"Characterize?"

"Casual, determined, angry?"

"I don't know, sort of . . . cold and flat, I guess. The only time it changed, got a little angry, was after I put him on hold. Oh, and there was something funny about his voice."

"Funny how?"

"Well, kind of slurred. But not as if he was drunk."

"Speech impediment?"

"Something like that."

"You said you put him on hold. Why?"

"Janet's other call came through — call forwarding."

"At what point in the conversation?"

"We hadn't been talking long," Ms. Sukimoto said, "less than a minute. I think I'd just said I couldn't help him, I wasn't Spook's caseworker, and he was saying

146

couldn't I just give him some idea of where he could find Spook."

"How long'd you keep him on hold?"

"Oh, a couple of minutes. I had to take a message for Janet."

"And he didn't like being kept waiting."

"No. I didn't mean to but I guess I cut him off kind of abruptly to answer the other call. He said something about that, told me not to do it again — don't put him on hold again because he was calling long distance."

"Those were his words, long distance?"

Wrinkles appeared in Ms. Sukimoto's brow. "Actually, that wasn't what he said. He said he was calling from . . . some county. What was it? Oh, right. Mono County. 'I'm calling from Mono County.' "

"Is that all? No specific location?"

"That's all."

Mono County was in the eastern part of the state, in the high desert along the Nevada line. Large in terms of square miles, but with a relatively small population. There were no towns of any size, and only one or two with more than five thousand inhabitants.

Not much of a lead without additional information. "Older but not ancient" and the speech impediment indicated he might not be the same mole-cheeked man who'd been asking Spook's whereabouts among the homeless along lower Potrero. Which meant what, if that were the case? Two men looking for Spook for different reasons, or for the same reason independently? Or was there some sort of connection between the two?

11

Jake Runyon

It took him three and a half days to track down Big Dog.

He might've cut that time in half if he'd been able to devote all his working hours to the task. But Tamara Corbin had given him a handful of interview assignments on another case that took up all of Wednesday afternoon and half of Thursday. Routine work — white collar offices in the city, an upper middle-class home in Palo Alto. He preferred the streets, bleakness and all. His meat, his comfort zone.

He found out a couple of things on the Spook investigation before he found Big Dog. One was what Pete Snyder had told him, the only new information he'd gotten out of anybody at Visuals, Inc. The other came from one of the homeless who'd known Spook, the one called Pinkeye. Why he had that street name Runyon never did find out. Both his eyes were brown, milky with cataracts, the whites more or less clear, and there wasn't anything else pink about him. Big, loose-jointed black man, face mostly hidden behind a grizzled, gray prophet's beard. And eager enough to talk once he had two dollars of Runyon's money tucked away in a saggy pants pocket. He knew Big Dog, too, well enough to steer clear of him. ("Bad dude, cut your throat for a dime and drink your blood afterward.") Couldn't help with Big Dog's whereabouts; his information had to do with Spook.

"I wonder what happened to his stuff," he said.

"What stuff?"

"His stuff, man. Everybody out here's got stuff."

"Police didn't find anything on him."

"Sure they didn't. Don't keep your stuff on you, not if you want to *keep* it."

"Where, then?"

"Got to have a hidey hole," Pinkeye said. "Everybody got a hidey hole somewhere. You got one yourself, I bet."

"You know where Spook's was?"

"No idea, man. You tell anybody where you got your stuff hid, ain't gonna be yours for long."

"What kind of stuff did Spook have?"

"Bright and pretty, that's what he collected. Sidewalks, gutter, garbage cans, Dumpsters . . . scoured 'em all. All kinds of bright and pretty."

"Such as? Give me an example."

"One time," Pinkeye said, "I seen him pick up a gold earring. Yeah. One big old gold earring, right off the sidewalk. Not real gold, just a bright and pretty, but the way he grinned and hopped around you'd've thought it was. I asked him what was he gonna do with it. 'Give it to Dot,' he says."

"Dot. His ghost woman?"

"Yeah. One of old Spook's head people. 'She likes pretty things,' he says. 'Gonna give it to her, she'll look real pretty, maybe she'll forgive me.' "

"Forgive him for what?"

"Wouldn't say. Talked *to* his head people but wouldn't talk *about* 'em."

"So you figure he kept the earring with the rest of his stuff."

"What else, man? Dot wasn't no real woman. Can't give no bright and pretty to somebody only lives inside your head."

Runyon had gone back to Visuals, Inc. and talked to the client and to Meg Lawton. Both were surprised to hear that

151

Spook had had a hidey hole, collected shiny objects; he'd never said anything on either subject. Franklin Square had been next. No help from Delia or any of the other homeless who hung out there. No help from anybody else he talked to.

After he finished up the last of the interviews on Wednesday afternoon, he drove to the Potrero neighborhood and picked up where he'd left off, widening the radius of his search. Lower Potrero from Duboce to Twentieth on the north; all the way past Highway 280 to Third and the area called Dogpatch on the south; back north and then west toward Army. Street people, liquor store clerks, employees and inhabitants of greasy spoons and bars, plus a homeless shelter and a soup kitchen he hadn't tried before. And finally, midday on Friday, all the legwork paid off.

Liquor store with heavily barred windows, near Mission on Twenty-fifth; a thin man of Middle Eastern descent behind a counter protected by a wall of bullet-proof glass. "Him, that one," the man said when Runyon described Big Dog. "He better not come in here anymore. I don't want his money, I told him I don't want to see his face again."

"When was that? The last time you saw him?"

"Only one time. The night before last. He comes in drunk, staggering, he wants to buy a bottle of Jack Daniel's. I tell him I don't have any Jack Daniel's, he starts yelling. Dirty words, dirty names. Calls me an obscenity Muslim, an Arab terrorist. I am not a Muslim, I am not an Arab, I am not a terrorist. I tell him I am Jordanian, but he keeps right on calling me names. I tell him to get out or I call the police. He keeps on yelling obscenities. So I pick up the phone, I call the police, and then he leaves before they come."

"Any idea where he came from or where he went?"

"I don't know, I don't want to know."

"He wanted a bottle of Jack Daniel's, you said?"

"Jack Daniel's. In this neighborhood."

"So he must've had money to pay for it."

"Yes, he had money. He waved his money, twenty dollars he waved while he called me an obscenity Arab Muslim terrorist."

Runyon found two other liquor stores in the teeming, mostly Latino neighborhood. Big Dog had been in both, had bought a fifth of Jack Daniel's in one three days ago, the only bottle of Jack they'd had in stock; the second store hadn't had any and he'd verbally abused the clerk there too. That placed him in the general vicinity. Another hour of canvassing, and Runyon located a panhandler on Twenty-third and Shotwell who admitted, in exchange for the usual cash dole, that he'd seen Big Dog in the neighborhood recently.

"He's a mean son of a bitch, drunk or sober. Knocked down an old guy got in his way the other night, just knocked him down and kicked him like he was a cat. Why'd he hafta move in on *this* neighborhood, for Chrissake?"

"How long's he been here?"

"Week or so. Too freakin' long."

"Ever see him before that?"

"No. What you want with him?"

Runyon said, "You know where he hangs?"

"I think he's got a room at the Commerce."

"Commerce? Doesn't sound like a shelter."

"Nah. Roach hotel. One of them residence joints."

"Address?"

"Right up on the next block. But he

probly ain't there now."

"No?"

"I see him goin' into Fat Tony's a while ago."

"Fat Tony's is what, a bar?"

"Pool joint. Tobacco and pool. Twenty-fourth, near Mission."

"How long ago?"

"Right before I come down here and I ain't been here long."

Fat Tony's turned out to be a storefront with a dirt-streaked plate glass window that you couldn't see through clearly until you stood up close. Long, gloomy, droplit interior, counter and cases and shelves of tobacco along one wall, the rest of the space taken up with pool and snooker tables in decent repair. Only one of the tables was in use, by two Latino men. The only other occupant was a huge blob of a man on a ladderback stool.

On the wall behind the fat man was what looked like a blow-up of a cartoonish Christmas card. Santa Claus on a snowy rooftop, his sleigh and reindeer parked to one side, the animals lying down in their traces, the words SEASON'S GREETINGS FROM SANTA in scraggly letters in the snow. It seemed out of place in these surroundings until Runyon got close enough

155

to see the details. St. Nick was standing in partial profile, a stream of urine coming from his unbuttoned trousers, writing his holiday message in dirty yellow. Right. Not out of place at all.

The fat man said, "Ain't that a pisser?"

"What?"

"Cartoon." Rumbling sounds rolled out of the massive chest. "A real pisser, ain't it?"

"Hilarious," Runyon said. "I'm looking for Big Dog."

"Who?"

Runyon described him. The fat man's jolly little smile turned upside down. "Yeah, he was here. Half hour ago, maybe."

"First time, or he been in before?"

"Couple times before."

"Buy tobacco? Shoot pool?"

"Neither. Don't buy nothing, ain't a player. Asshole drunk. Pig-dirty bum."

"Then why does he come in?"

"Lookin' for one of my regulars. Pablo."

"Pablo who?"

"Just Pablo. Another asshole. Fuckin' butcher, what I hear."

"Butcher?"

"Raw meat salesman. You dig what I mean?"

Runyon nodded. "What kind of raw meat?"

"What kind you think?"

"Child porn?"

"What I hear. Little kiddies. I hate that shit, man."

"Makes two of us. Big Dog one of Pablo's customers?"

Shrug. "One and one adds up to two, don't it?"

"Where can I find Pablo?"

"Works in a tacqueria on Mission. Grease cook."

"That where you sent Big Dog today?"

"What I told him, same as you."

Runyon pried loose the name and general location of the tacqueria. Then he said, "If you hate what this butcher peddles, why do you let him hang out in here?"

"Why?" Fat Tony seemed surprised at the question. "I got to make a living, too, don't I?"

The tacqueria was a hole-in-the-wall, overheated by the big cookstove and ovens behind the serving counter, the air clogged with the smells of chile peppers and fried lard. Two of the eight tables had customers. At one an old man was finishing a burrito in careful little bites. And against the rear wall, a big man sat hunched vulturelike over a table strewn with plates, beer bottles, and spilled food. He had a ratty red and green wool cap on his head, wore what might have been a recently purchased secondhand rain slicker with the collar pulled up and new, thick-soled black shoes. The slicker already had foodstains on it, some dried, some fresh. He clenched a dripping taco in one hand, was using two fingers of the other hand to scoop up beans and shovel them into his mouth.

Feeding time for Big Dog.

Runyon stopped a couple of paces from the table, stood sizing him up. A brute, all right. Inch or two over six feet, bullet head, thick neck, running to sloppy fat from booze and poor diet. The close-set, squinty eyes and the looseness of his features said he was as stupid as he was mean. Bad news anywhere. On the street, among the weak and the down-and-out, he'd be a holy terror.

It took close to thirty seconds for him to realize he had company. His head swung up slowly, the little pig eyes focused on Runyon; words and taco sauce dribbled out through a half-chewed mouthful. "What the fug you lookin' at?"

"You, Big Dog."

"You know me? I don't know you. Fug off."

"We need to talk."

"Can't you see I'm eatin'?"

Runyon sat down across from him.

"I told you fug off, not sit down. You want your head busted?"

"Like Spook got his head busted?"

". . . Huh?"

"Spook. Somebody busted his head with a bullet."

Confusion bunched the coarse features. He shook himself like an animal.

"Maybe you didn't do it, but could be you know who did. Who and why."

Big Dog's reaction caught him off guard. He expected denial, and he was ready for anger and aggression; he'd learned how to handle slow-witted thugs in his years working the Seattle waterfront. But what replaced Big Dog's confusion was fear, and what he did then was motivated by it. He howled, "I ain't goin' to jail!" and shoved the table hard into Runyon's midriff, driving him backward, and then lurched to his feet and barreled out of the tacqueria at a staggering run.

By the time Runyon kicked free of the table and chair and reached the sidewalk outside, Big Dog was lumbering around the corner onto Twenty-second Street. A light rain was falling and the pavement was slick; Runyon had no trouble with his footing, but Big Dog was clumsy and at least half drunk and the soles on his new shoes were still smooth. He slipped cutting across the street, went down and skidded on hands and knees into the far curb. The fall and the time it took him to scramble up and get moving again allowed Runyon to halve the distance between them. The separation was less than thirty yards when Big Dog plunged into a one-way alley mid-block, went charging down its narrow length between close-packed rows of parked cars.

Runyon caught up to him halfway along, grabbed hold of the belt on his rain slicker and tried to yank him to a stop. Big Dog twisted free, stumbled sideways into a parked car, caromed off and wheeled to face him. His eyes were wild; taco juice and drool gave his wide-open mouth a bloody look. "Get away from me," he yelled, "I ain't goin' to jail!"

Instead Runyon moved in on him. He ducked a flailing arm, jabbed stiffened knuckles into the soft fat under the bulging sternum. Would've followed that up with judo shots to the throat and neck, hurt him enough to subdue him, except that Big Dog's new shoes slid again on the wet pavement and the belly blow connected only glancingly. It took away some but not all of his wind, left him enough strength and mobility to flail out again. Runyon tried to duck away, but he was in too close by then and vulnerable.

The big fist smacked him solidly on the left ear, sent him reeling into another of the cars. Its front bumper struck him mid-thigh, threw him up over the hood. He rolled down between that car and the one in front, banging his head. Both his vision and his faculties went out of whack; he was only dimly aware of hitting the pavement.

For a few seconds his head was full of ringing and roaring and he couldn't move. His face was upturned; he felt nothing, then he felt the rain, then he was aware of pain — head, thigh, shoulder. And then his motor responses returned and he was clawing up the front of the car, onto his feet again. He backhanded his eyes clear, blinked them into focus as he came out limping from between the cars.

Big Dog was running again. Down at the end of the block, not looking back. Around the corner and gone.

Runyon let him go. He wasn't hurt

161

much, but he didn't see any point in continuing the chase. The fact that Big Dog had run told him some of what he wanted to know. The rest he could find out by other means. Or the SFPD could. Wherever Big Dog went now, it wouldn't be any place where he could hide for very long.

12

Jake Runyon

The Commerce was two stories of colorless wood and dirty windows piled atop a row of storefronts. The entrance was a single door set into a shallow alcove, the words COMMERCE HOTEL — ROOMS BY WEEK, MONTH painted on its glass panel. Alongside the latch was a button and a card that said you had to ring for admittance after 9 P.M.

Runyon walked by slowly without turning in. Across the street and down a short way was a bakery and coffee shop with a long front window; he went over there, bought a cup of tea, took it to one of the stools at a counter that ran along below the rain-spotted window. From there he had a reasonably unobstructed view of the hotel entrance.

He had come straight back here, so Big Dog hadn't had time to get to the Commerce ahead of him. He might not come back at all, as scared as he was. Runyon gave it half an hour, nursing his tea; nobody went into the Commerce, nobody came out. He left the bakery's warmth and crossed the street again.

A bell jangled when he opened the glass-paneled door of the hotel, jangled again as he shut it behind him. Postage-stamp lobby with nothing in it — no chairs or tables, no adornments of any kind. The front desk, if you could call it that, was an even smaller cubicle enclosed by a wood-and-glass partition. This was a neighborhood of cages within cages. One of hundreds in a nationwide network of urban zoos: some animals locked in, others allowed to roam free, and a tossup as to which group had the most dangerous predators.

Framed behind the glass of this cage was a woman perched on an office chair, the kind that you could crank to adjust the height. This one was up as high as it would go, so that her breasts seemed to be resting on the inside counter. She was something to look at in there, like an exotic and faintly repulsive creature on display. Indeterminate age, anywhere from thirty to fifty. Ropy black hair pulled back so tightly from her face that the skin looked stretched to the splitting point along temples and forehead. Tall, thin body, dead-white skin, blank eyes, too much lipstick and rouge. Bloodless, lifeless — a victim in a vampire movie. Junkie, probably. Smack or crystal meth. The long-sleeved shirt would be to cover the needle tracks on her arms.

"Yeah?" she said. Her mouth barely moved. The empty eyes didn't move at all.

"What room is Big Dog in?"

"Who?"

Runyon described him, including the rain slicker and new shoes.

"Big Dog, hell," she said. "Big prick. Not in."

"I'll wait for him."

"No waiting here."

"What's his room number?"

"Guests only upstairs."

"What name is he registered under?"

Blank stare.

"How long has he been staying here?"

Blank stare.

It was like trying to communicate with an animated corpse. Stoned? Those empty eyes said it was likely. He weighed options. Money was the obvious pry bar, but if he put a bill of any denomination into the tray in the glass partition, she was liable to make it disappear without giving him any-thing in return. Silent intimidation or threats wouldn't get the job done, either. Her cage, her advantage.

"He's in trouble, lady. Big trouble."

Blank stare.

"A prick, you said. So why protect him?"

Blank stare.

"Be smart and protect yourself. You don't want his kind of trouble to rub off on you."

"Cop?"

"You could say that."

"Badge."

Waste of time showing her his temporary California license, but he did it anyway. Colleen had given him a leather holder for his Washington state license one birth-day; he flipped it open, held it up near the glass.

"Bullshit," she said.

"You think so?"

"Go away."

Runyon said, "Murder."

"What?"

"You heard me. Murder."

"More bullshit."

"Big Dog's involved in a street killing. Cops are as interested in talking to him as I am. I'll go call them, report that you're shielding him, might be mixed up in the homicide yourself."

Blank stare.

"If they don't arrest you for that, there's always a drug charge. Withdrawal in a jail cell's no picnic, lady, if you don't already know it. Sometimes they don't pay any attention to your screams."

He walked away on the last sentence — five steps to the door. He had his hand on the latch when she said, "Wait."

Back to the cage. She hadn't moved; her eyes and her expression were as blank as before. But her body language said he'd touched the right nerve.

"Well?"

"Nine," she said. "Second floor."

"What name?"

A blue-veined hand snaked out, flipped open a register. "Joe Smith."

"Sure. How long's he been here?"

"Few days."

"Renting by the week?"

"Month. Paid in advance."

"One month?"

"Deaf? Month, in advance."

"Paid how?"

"Cash. No credit cards."

"What's the monthly rate?"

"Two and a quarter."

167

Two hundred twenty-five dollars, cash. Drinking cheap wine with Spook in an alley a few weeks ago; drinking good sour mash whiskey since he moved into this neighborhood. Paying for a room one month in advance. Wearing a recently bought rain slicker and a pair of new shoes. Where did a homeless alcoholic get the kind of money he was throwing around?

"Where does he hang out when he's not here?"

"Who knows."

"Calls for him? Visitors?"

"No."

"I need to look at his room," Runyon said.

"Guests only upstairs."

"Ten minutes, no more."

"Guests only upstairs."

"Suppose I rent your passkey."

"Rent?"

"Ten minutes, ten dollars."

"Twenty."

"Ten. And nobody finds out I was here, cops included."

The corpse pose lasted until he opened his wallet, removed a ten and flattened it against the glass. Then the veined hand snaked out again and a scarlet nail tapped the partition tray.

"Passkey first," he said, "then you get the money."

"No."

"Same-time exchange, then."

". . . Okay."

So he went through the ritual with her, putting the money into the tray and holding onto it with two fingers while she did likewise with the passkey; taking hold of the key while she pinched the other end of the sawbuck, like a four-handed tug of war; both of them pulling and letting go simultaneously. She squinted at the bill, as though she thought it might be counterfeit, then made it vanish inside the front of her white shirt.

"Ten minutes," she said.

"Don't worry. Neither of us wants me around any longer than that."

There was no elevator. Runyon climbed dust-carpeted stairs, found his way to a door at the rear with the number 9 painted on it. The passkey let him into a twelve-foot-square box that reeked of stale booze, stale food, stale tobacco, and human excretion. Blanket-wadded single bed, tiny nightstand, scratched-up bureau, one rickety chair. Scatter of empty liquor bottles, a tuna fish can full of cigarette butts, remnants of fast-food meals that had already attracted roaches — two of them scurried away when he switched on the naked ceiling bulb — and a filthy knapsack propped in one corner. Cold in there; the Commerce was the kind of place where the heat would be turned on for the legal minimum each day and not a minute longer.

Bare-bones survival living at two twenty-five a month. One step up from the streets; at least Spook's doorway at Visuals, Inc. had been free. This was what Big Dog had aspired to, what he'd spent part of his windfall on — one month in a cold, foul-smelling roach box and subsistence on hard liquor and junk food. Drunk, drifter, bully, bum. And a probable felon besides. The kind of borderline human who gave homelessness a bad name.

Runyon went over and squatted by the knapsack. Its straps were loose; he sifted through the pockets. No firearm of any kind, but plenty of testimony to Big Dog's character. In addition to a scant few articles of filthy clothing, he found a cracked roach pipe, a switchblade knife with a broken blade, and a tattered envelope that contained half a dozen pawed-over glossies depicting the nastier acts of child pornography. He stared to rip up the photos, changed his mind and stuffed them back into the envelope, put the envelope into his coat pocket.

He turned the knapsack around to get at the pouch on the other side. Only one thing in there: a dirty cloth sack home-made out of what had once been a small pillowcase. Its contents rattled when he lifted it out. He undid the crude draw-string, spread the cloth open.

String of colored beads. Tiny brass cat. Half a dozen new pennies. Top to a simu-lated gold fountain pen. Woman's compact made of scratched silver plate. Shiny copper pipe fitting. Pair of fingernail clip-pers on a silver chain. And a single gold-filled hoop earring with a broken fastener.

Bright and pretty. Spook's stash.

There were two other items in the bag. One was an old, torn, edgeworn Valen-tine's Day card on the front of which was a tufted gold and red heart enclosing the words I LOVE YOU. Inside, below the usual sentimental message, was an inked signa-ture that read *Your Dottie*. The other item was a piece of heavy, slick paper folded into a two-inch square. It had been opened and refolded so many times that the paper had begun to separate along the creases. He spread it out carefully on the filthy carpet.

Page of black-and-white, head-and-shoulders studio portraits from an old school yearbook. Mix of some forty teenage boys and girls, twenty on each side, their names printed below each photo. One of the portraits had a crude heart drawn around it, like the heart on the Valentine's card, in smudged pencil: a dark-haired, attractive girl named Dorothy Lightfoot. Dorothy . . . Dot.

There was nothing on either side of the page to identify the school or year. No writing or other marks. And none of the boys was named Luke or Duke or anything similar. Or Snow.

Runyon refolded the page, tucked it into a different pocket. His watch said he'd been there a little more than eight minutes. He said aloud, " 'And when the big dog comes home, he'll tell you what the little dog done.' " But Big Dog wouldn't be coming home, most likely. And when he did turn up again, it'd be the SFPD he told his story to.

Runyon had had as much of this place as he could stand. He pulled the drawstring on the cloth, returned the sack to the pocket where he'd found it, stood the knapsack in its original place. The only reason he locked the door behind him when he left was to keep the other residents from stealing the knapsack.

Downstairs, the vampire woman was still doing nothing except sitting on her cranked-up chair and staring blankly into space. The dead eyes shifted to him as he approached her cage, watched him drop the passkey into the tray. Then, slowly and deliberately, she gave him the finger. Animal trick, like the baboon he'd once seen mooning a crowd of onlookers at the Seattle zoo. He ignored it, went out into the dirty streets and the clean rain.

13

I was out of the office most of Thursday. After Tamara and I wrapped up the report for McCone Investigations, I took it over to Pier 24-½ and hand-delivered it to Ted Smalley. Then I spent an hour and a half with a Maritime Plaza attorney who specialized in felony appeals cases and who was looking to hire a small agency on a retainer basis to do his investigative work. I thought the interview went pretty well, but with lawyers you can never be sure of anything. Early afternoon I played hooky again and finished my Christmas shopping at Union Square. Nokia cell phone for Emily, four-ounce bottle of expensive French perfume for Kerry, a couple of multicolored silk scarves for Tamara, and another overload of crowd-and-Christmas commercialism for me.

It was nearly five when I got back to O'Farrell Street, just missing Jake Runyon. He'd found and had some trouble with Big Dog, Tamara informed me; he'd also uncovered a lead on Spook's background. She filled me in before she handed over the heavily creased page of photos.

"Runyon okay?" I asked.

"Lump on his head and a sore ear. Tough dude."

"And a good investigator."

"Man knows judo, you believe it?"

"Good for him. So you like him better now?"

"I always liked him. *You* the one didn't want to hire him."

"Well, you didn't seem to like either of us much, earlier in the week."

"Already said I was sorry. My bad, and I'm keeping it out the office from now on."

True enough. She'd settled down quite a bit since Monday, lost some of her edge and got her frustrations under control. But the Horace situation was still eating her up inside. And she was still living at her sister's.

I said, "So Big Dog figures to be blackmailing whoever shot Spook."

"How it looks."

"Dangerous game when the mark's already killed once."

"Dude's got two brain cells, Runyon says."

"Two questions come to mind. Does Big

175

Dog know the motive? Does he know Spook's real identity?"

"Make it three," she said. "How'd he ID the shooter?"

"Make it four. How'd he get hold of Spook's stash?"

"Make it five. Anything in the stash that wasn't with the rest of the stuff in the knapsack?"

"Might be the answer to number three, if there was. Something that named or pointed to the shooter. What's Runyon's take on all this?"

"He's not guessing."

I looked over the sheet of photographs, studied the one of the girl named Dorothy Lightfoot encased in the penciled heart. "High school yearbook. Graduating class, you think?"

"Hard to tell. Nothing to ID the school or location."

"Could be Mono County, if there's any connection to the phone call to Human Services."

"I can find out. Be easier if we knew the time frame."

"Hairstyles ought to give some idea."

"White kids, all of 'em," Tamara said. "I never did pay much attention to white kids' do's. Before my time, anyway. Got to be pretty old, that page."

"Twenty years, at least. Maybe twenty-five or thirty."

"Doesn't narrow it down much."

"No, but I think I can get it narrowed down."

"Yeah? How?"

"Kerry. Advertising people get paid to notice hairstyles, clothes, things like that, past as well as present." I folded and pocketed the sheet. "Either you or Runyon contact SFPD with all this?"

"He did," she said. "Stopped to see Jack Logan on his way back here. Only thing he held out was the page of photos . . . same as you'd've done."

"In my younger days, anyhow."

"One other thing he gave the lieutenant, also same as you would've — that envelope of kiddie porn. No more raw meat for Pablo. He's gonna be spoiled meat pretty soon."

Right. The two types of felons cops hate more than any other are child molesters and kiddie-porn vendors. They'd put Pablo out of commission fast. Big Dog, too, but only if finding him proved easy. Otherwise, even with the new reforms in the department, they'd let the case slide again in favor of higher priority squeals.

I said as much to Tamara. She said, "Runyon's take, too. Big Dog's still loose by this time tomorrow, he wants to go back out on the streets and see if maybe he can help put a leash on him."

"What'd you tell him?"

"Okay with me, but I'd check with you."

"Iffy."

"Runyon said he'd do the job on his own time."

"The hell he did."

"Man's a workaholic. Sound familiar?"

"Uh-huh."

"Only difference is, you got a life and he doesn't. Nobody to go home to and a grown son who hates his guts, you know what I'm sayin'?"

"Sounds like compassion."

"Well, I been thinking about the man. About a lot of things. I got bad, but I also got people who care — family, friends. Folks like Runyon, they got all the bad and none of the good. I figure the least we can do is give him anything reasonable he asks for."

"Be his friends as well as his employers."

"Yeah, well, why not?"

I felt paternal as hell toward her in that moment. Tamara Corbin — from hostile streetwise college kid to mature businesswoman in less than five years. I'd had a small hand in it and it made me feel proud, the way her real father must feel about her.

On impulse I went over and put my arm around her and kissed her on the cheek.

"Hey, why'd you do that?"

I grinned and said, "Why not?"

"Nineteen seventy-seven," Kerry said.

"Come on. The exact year?"

"Want to make a little bet?"

"You only looked at the photos for about two minutes."

"I don't need any more time. I could give you a four- or five-year window — late seventies to early eighties — but 'seventy-seven seems right. The photos were probably taken in the late fall of 'seventy-six, a few months before the yearbook was released."

"Now you're really guessing."

"Want to make a bet?" she asked again.

"No way I'd ever bet against that smug look of yours."

"I don't have a smug look."

"Go look in the mirror. All right, tell me why you're so sure. Dazzle me with your deductive powers."

"I should've been a detective, huh?

Stolen some of your thunder?"

"God forbid. Come on, give."

"I worked on my high school yearbook," she said. "Photos are usually taken in the fall of the year before the book comes out. Three or four months' lead time, to allow for layout, proofreading, printing. *Capito?*"

"*Capito.* But that doesn't explain how you can pinpoint an exact year."

" 'Charlie's Angels,' for one thing."

"Who?"

"Number one rated TV show in the late seventies. Three beautiful women private eyes who worked for a mysterious boss named Charlie."

"Never heard of it."

"You're kidding. Famous jiggle show."

"What's a jiggle show?"

"Now I know you've heard *that* term before."

"If I have, I didn't internalize it."

"They didn't wear bras, bounced when they moved. Jiggle show."

"Oh. Sexy stuff."

"You sure you never watched the show?"

"You know I don't watch episodic TV."

One of her analytical looks. "Sometimes I could swear you're putting me on. You can't be that far out of the mainstream, can you?"

"Why can't I? The only things on the tube that interest me are sports and old movies. And I like my sex up close and personal, not bouncing and jiggling on a screen."

"That much I know isn't a put on."

"So what about this 'Charlie's Angels' show?"

"Well, one of the actresses was Farrah Fawcett. Blonde, wore her hair in a long, distinctive style. Waves, feathers . . . never mind." Kerry poked the grubby page under my nose and tapped one of the photos. "This style. It was all the rage back then. Three of the girls here have the Farrah look."

"Okay, I get it now. That explains the window but not the specific year."

" 'Charlie's Angels' first aired in the fall of 'seventy-six," she said patiently, although the patience seemed to be wearing a little thin. "A lot of girls adopted the Farrah look right away — more then than later, when the novelty began to wear off."

"That's not conclusive evidence."

"Not conclusive, no, but —"

"So admit it, you're just guessing."

"I am not guessing!"

"Then give me conclusive proof the year is nineteen seventy-seven."

"The pin," she said.

"What pin?"

"One of the girls is wearing a pin. Didn't you notice it?"

"No. Which girl?"

The page came at me again; she almost banged me on the nose with it. A finger came around and jabbed a photo near the bottom. "This girl. This pin."

I squinted. Pin, all right, on a chubby girl's black sweater. Up close, now that I was focused on it, it looked vaguely familiar.

"Looks vaguely familiar," I said.

Kerry said, not quite in one of her exasperated growls, "Nineteen seventy-six. What does that mean to you?"

"Doesn't mean anything to me."

"Don't start that again."

"Don't start what again?"

"The year nineteen seventy-six," she said in one of her exasperated growls, "what happened that year, why is it historically important, what did it represent?"

"Oh," I said. "Bicentennial."

"The light dawns. That's right, it was the Bicentennial. And a lot of people, especially in small towns, young people all over the country, celebrated by wearing Bicentennial pins. The girl in this photo is wearing a Bicentennial pin. After nineteen seventy-six, when the Bicentennial ended, hardly anybody wore the pins because there was no longer any reason to. *Quod erat demonstrandum.*"

"What does that mean?" I said.

"Q.E.D."

"Huh?"

"Gahh," she said.

"What does *that* mean?"

She folded the sheet carefully, tucked it into my shirt pocket, glared at me, said, "You can be a pain in the ass sometimes, you know that?" and walked out of the room.

I sat down in my chair and tried to figure out what I'd done to set her off like that. Nothing, I decided. Chalk it up to the fact that women are emotional creatures. Emotional and volatile and unpredictable and often unreadable, not anything like men.

Give Tamara enough of a starting point, she can find out just about anything in what she calls cyberspace. Fast, a lot faster than by dint of the creaky old methods I'd relied on for so many years. First thing Friday morning she took the three slim leads we had — Mono County, the page from what Kerry insisted was a 1977 high school yearbook, and the only Dorothy on the two-sided page of photos — and by early afternoon she had made connections and pulled up facts that answered some questions and opened up a potential can of worms.

The page of photos was from the High Desert Municipal High School yearbook in Aspen Creek, a town of 2,500 residents not far from Mono Lake in Mono County. And Kerry had been right, by God, about the date being 1977. Dorothy Lightfoot had graduated that year, with honors.

Tamara checked public records on file in Bridgeport, the Mono County seat. No birth certificate for Dorothy Lightfoot, but a marriage license had been issued to her and a man named Anthony Colton in the spring of 1979. If the union had produced any offspring, the birth had taken place elsewhere.

There was another certificate on file in Mono, one that was a little surprising. On August 19, 1985, Dorothy Lightfoot Colton had died in Aspen Creek. The death certificate did not list the cause.

"Twenty-five years, six months," Tamara said. "Dag, that's my age, almost exactly. Twenty-five's too young to die."

"Any age is too young to die," I said.

"I guess. But twenty-five . . ."

"Accident, maybe."

"Let's see if there's an obit anywhere online."

There wasn't. Aspen Creek was too small to have a newspaper, and none of the other Mono sheets had the staff, time, or money to put their back issue files on the Internet.

I said, "Find out if Anthony Colton still lives in Aspen Creek or anywhere else in the county."

He didn't. Nor did anybody else named Colton.

"Try the Lightfoot name."

While she was doing that, Runyon came in. We'd had him out doing legwork on the engineering employee case. He gave me a quick report on his findings, then I filled him in on what Tamara had learned so far.

He asked, "Big Dog picked up yet?"

"I checked in with Logan a little while ago. Still at large."

"So it's okay if I see what I can do?"

"Go ahead."

Pretty soon Tamara said, "Two hits on Lightfoot, neither one in Aspen Creek. Robert in Bridgeport, George in Lee Vining." She'd been using Big Hugs for that search, a website that had been created to help trace adoptive parents and then expanded into other search areas. Through a subscription to that site, you can find out, among other things, the addresses of ninety percent of the U.S. population.

Runyon said, "How about checking the Snow name?"

"Good idea."

Very good idea, as it turned out. It produced a second surprise.

One Vernon Snow, age 64, had died in Aspen Creek on August 19, 1985 — the same day as Dorothy Lightfoot Colton.

"Dot and Mr. Snow," Tamara said. "We got us a connection, for sure."

"What we need now is the cause of both deaths," I said. "One of the papers up there must have something on file — obits, a news story if the deaths were related or anything other than natural."

"After three Friday afternoon. Not much chance of getting anybody to check files for us in a hurry."

"With the weekend, it might take days." Small-town newspaper offices were generally closed on weekends, and always seemed to be understaffed and too busy to respond quickly to out-of-town requests. The same was true of small-town, rural county libraries; their hours were shorter, their staffs even smaller.

Tamara ran a "death sweep" on Anthony Colton. That's another of Big Hugs' online search services: you can find out the date and place of death of ninety percent of American citizens deceased during the past fifty years or more, using the individual's birth date and place of birth as a starting point. Anthony Colton of Mono County, CA, wasn't one of them, however. Either he was still alive or among the ten percent whose deaths, for one reason or another, had gone unrecorded.

Running a criminal background check on the four names would've been easy enough if Tamara's friend Felicia had been on duty in SFPD's communications department. But she wasn't. Civilians, in which class private detectives fall, can't access National Crime Information Center computer files, and without specific details Tamara couldn't pull up the information on her own without doing some illegal hacking. The check would have to wait until Monday morning, when Felicia was due back on the job.

Runyon said, "I could drive up to Mono County, see what I can find out over the weekend."

Tamara and I both gave him a look. "Mono's way up along the Nevada line," I said. "Six or seven hundred miles, round trip. Three or four days altogether."

"I wouldn't mind, if you don't need me on Monday."

I considered it. "Well . . . it might save us some time, at that. Always easier to dig out details in person. But the client might not want to authorize the extra expense."

"I could call him," Tamara said.

"What's the schedule look like first of next week?"

"Christmas week. Not much happening."

"All right. Call Steve Taradash, see what he says."

Taradash said okay. So we said the same to Runyon. If the workaholic wanted to feed his habit with a twelve-hundred mile roundtrip drive, might as well let him do it. God knew I'd done enough of that kind of feeding myself over the long haul.

14

Tamara

She trudged up the stairs to Claudia's flat, keyed open the door — and there was Horace, big as life, bigger, all duded up in a sport coat and tie, sitting on the damn sofa with her sister.

Tamara stopped short. Been a long day and she was tired, she was cold and damp from a two-block walk in the rain, and she was hungry. All she wanted was something to eat, a long hot bath, and a book that'd put her to sleep in less than ten pages. Instead, just as she was starting to drag herself out of the glooms, get her head together, she had this to deal with.

She said to Claudia, "Sister Judas."

"Now don't fly off the handle —"

"How many times did I ask you, beg you, don't let no sweet-talkin' longhair musicians come round here?"

"Don't blame Claudia," Horace said. He

was on his big feet now. "I talked her into it. We're both hurting, Tamara, we have to get this situation resolved."

She ignored him. Damn room looked like a stage set for a dumb-ass holiday play. Lights turned down low, gas fire going, Claudia's tree all lit up and twinkling blue and green in the bay window, Christmas CD humming and jingling in the background. He'd talked her into it. Sure, right. Looked like they'd planned it together. Sister Judas and the Cello King, co-conspirators.

"Where're the caterers?" she said. "Call 'em in. I can sure use a glass of bubbly."

"Caterers?" Claudia said. "What're you talking about?"

"Never mind."

Horace said, "Tamara, baby . . ."

"Who's that barking? Some stray? Better let him out before he pees all over your Persian carpet."

"Please don't be a smartass about this. Can't you just sit down and talk things over with Horace like a responsible adult?"

"Horace who?"

Claudia sighed. Ever since they were kids she'd done a lot of sighing, usually over something Tamara said or did that she didn't approve of. She was four years older, ten pounds heavier, one shade darker, and as far as Tamara was concerned, two shades uglier. She was also a born-again vegan, wouldn't eat anything that wasn't grown organically and washed eleven times in purified water, didn't have enough sense of humor to stuff an olive, got her jollies reading obscure law precedents, refused to own a TV, and had a boyfriend who wasn't only another lawyer but an oreo with a tighter ass than hers. And she thought her little sis had problems.

"I'm outta here," Tamara said.

"No, you're not. You're going to stay put and have this out with Horace."

"Don't know anybody named Horace."

Another sigh. "I'm the one who's leaving. I have a date with Brian — I told you that this morning. We're going to *The Nutcracker*."

"You ask me, Brian ought to have his nuts cracked."

". . . What kind of thing is that to say?"

"I don't know what you see in that man. He must do something pretty terrific in bed, all I can figure."

"Tamara . . ."

"What's his idea of foreplay? Reading you one of his briefs?"

"That's enough!"

She looked somewhere between Claudia and Horace and said as if she were doing stand-up in front of a hostile audience, "What do you call two lawyers screwing? Anybody know?"

Breathless suspense while they waited for the punch line.

"Joint practice."

Thud.

She let go a sigh of her own, one that outdid Claudia's, threw her coat and purse onto one of the chairs, and stalked into the kitchen.

Unopened quart of milk she'd bought was in the fridge. She poured a tall glass full up, gulped it in three swallows. They were talking in the living room; she could hear the low mutter of voices but none of the words. Just as well. Who cared what they were saying? She wasn't hungry any more, but she found a cold chicken leg and stripped it to the bone in ten seconds flat. Drank more milk. Rummaged up a hunk of cheese and took it to the kitchen window, the one that overlooked Fell Street and the long strip of park. Panhandle looked deserted, lonesome, headlights on the cars passing and the house and street lights opposite on Oak all blurry and cold. Damn rain.

The mutter of voices stopped. She finished the cheese, stepped to the counter to finish the milk. Pretty quiet out there now. Both of them gone? Might as well find out.

Claudia was missing, but not Horace. Standing over in front of the fire, warming his chubby behind. All hangdog, like a big package somebody ordered and forgot to pick up. Whup, mixed metaphor. Language po-lice gonna get her sure.

God, she felt awful.

And not just from all the crap she'd eaten, either.

Horace was looking at her with those big eyes of his, fierce and sorrowful at the same time. Kick his sorry butt out the door. Ignore him. Go off on him again. But she couldn't make herself do any of those things. About all she could do was walk slow to the sofa and sink down on it.

Pretty soon he came over and lowered his bulk next to her. Better not get too close, better not touch her.

He didn't. He said in a choky voice, "Tamara."

"That's my name."

"You as miserable as I am?"

"Who says I'm miserable?"

"I do."

"Well, you're wrong. As usual."

"I know misery when I see it."

"Take a look in the mirror."

"In the mirror, and right here next to me."

"So what if I am? None of your business anymore."

"You'll always be my business."

"Sweet talkin' b.s."

"I couldn't stand it if I lost you, baby. I swear to God."

She closed her eyes. Leave it to him to say the one thing, in that choky voice, those brown eyes dripping sad, that could melt steel in her.

"I mean it," he said. "You know I love you."

"I hear you saying it."

"And you love me. Neither of us ever loved anybody else the way we love each other. You know that's the truth too."

"Sometimes love's not enough."

He laid his hand, gentle, on hers. "We belong together."

"Don't touch me."

He didn't move his hand. Move it for him, she thought . . . but she didn't.

"We belong together," he said again.

"I'm not going east with you."

"All right."

"Not gonna marry you either."

"All right."

"So what else is there?"

"There's now," he said.

"Now doesn't last very long. Then what?"

"Then we'll have tomorrow. Christmas. New Year's. One day at a time."

"That old song."

"Old song, true lyrics."

"Until there aren't any more days left."

"Everything ends, everybody's days run out. Better a little more time together than none at all, both of us alone and miserable."

"Horace, the philosopher."

"Horace, the man who loves you."

He slid nearer, tentatively. She didn't move. He put his arm around her, drew her against him, held her tight. She didn't pull away. Couldn't have if she'd tried. Big as a tree, warm, tender. Hers. And no denying she was his, like it or not. For the first time in a week she felt like bawling.

Damn man.

She lay with her head on his thick-furred chest, all limp and sweaty, her skin still tingling. Shouldn't've done that, she thought. Sex doesn't solve anything. But her body said different. Her body said she'd needed it as much as she ever had. Stress relief, misery relief. One thing you could say for Horace, he knew how to love a woman. Lord, did he know! But it was more than that. She knew it, even if she hated having to admit it to herself. *He* was what she really needed. All of him, every part, the good and the bad, in bed and out.

"Baby?" he said. "What're you thinking?"

"Not," she said.

"Liar. Thinking how good we are together, same as I was."

"In bed, maybe."

"In bed and every other way."

"I still won't change my mind."

"I'm not asking you to."

Liar, she thought. Not Horace — you, girl. Liar. Fool.

"There's only one thing I will ask," he said.

"What?"

"Don't give up on me. Don't give up on us."

She didn't have to think about her answer. There was only one answer, and no use trying to deny it or fight it any longer.

No more fool for the fool. Even if it meant giving in, giving up everything else she cared about — only one answer.

"I won't," she said.

15

Big Dog

The storage shed was a good place for a
stash, good place to hole up. Yeah, but not
for long. Cold, damp. Full of old toilets, old
sinks, all kinds of other plumbing crap. Full
of spiders and bugs, give you the fuggin' wil-
lies crawling over you in the dark. Nobody
around when he slipped in last night, nobody come in during the day. Heard their
trucks and them banging around out in the
yard until quitting time, but the door stayed
shut.

Plumbers didn't have no idea about the
corner of the back fence that peeled away
from the building wall. Or that you could
pop the storeroom lock in about two seconds flat. Spook, he'd been crazy but still
smarter than them plumbers. How'd he
find the place? Fuggin' radar or something.
Followed him that one night, couldn't
hardly believe it when old Spook peeled

the fence back, slipped into this here shed, come out again couple minutes later. Figured it had to be where his stash was. Took, what, five minutes to find it inside the busted crapper? Cloth sack full of junk except for the newspaper article and the business card. Yeah, that'd been his lucky day.

Only now his luck had squeezed down on him again. Never did last, none of his lucky times. Always something come along to screw it up. Like that cop yesterday, walked into Pablo's taco joint right outta nowhere. How'd he find out? Fuggin' cops. No more jail time for Big Dog. No way, man. Too many stinking cells in his life, too many faggots, moochers, assholes. Jump off a bridge before he'd go back behind bars.

Raining again. Beating on the shed roof, blowing in under the door. He rocked back and forth, shivering. Man, it was cold in here. Wasn't for the wool-lined rain slicker he'd picked up at Goodwill, and his new shoes, he'd of froze to death by now. Christ, he needed a drink. Hadn't been for that cop car cruising by this afternoon, on his way back from making the phone call, he'd of bought a jug. Should've risked it anyway. Should've swiped two bottles from that liquor store last night, not just one. One thing about booze, it kept you warm. Warm last night, freezin' his nuts off ever since the jug died early this A.M. He needed a drink bad, all right. Slide out early tonight, pick up a new supply before he met the money man? Nah, better not. Better keep a clear head until he got his hands on the cash.

Five thousand this time. What he should've asked for the first time. A lousy five hundred, what the hell was the matter with him? Too drunk to think straight that time. Five thousand bucks, yeah, that was the ticket. His ticket out of the rain, the fog, the cold, this fuggin' city. Someplace warm. Yeah, maybe down to Dago again. Good town, Dago. He'd had a ball there when he was in the navy. Before he smacked that smartass Chief Petty and they stuck him in the brig. Another piece of lousy luck. Well, he'd made some new luck today and this time it was gonna last. He'd be goin' back to Dago in style. Five thousand bucks, cash. Jesus, he'd never had that much green in his life. Never once in his whole fuggin' miserable life. Before that five hundred, only time he'd ever had more'n three loose bills in his kick was the pay he had coming when the

200

navy threw him out. And he'd blown that in one fuggin' weekend across the border in T-town.

When was it he'd scored the three bills? Oh, yeah, in Reno, back when he was still driving truck, before all the bastards kept getting in his way, bugging him while he was on a toot, back before he started smashing their faces and the cops kept haulin' his ass off to jail. No more of that, man, no more jail. Yeah, that time in Reno. Three hundred bucks on a blackjack run. Nothing but the best booze. Only he'd sucked down too much and that bitch whore, she'd rolled him in her crib while he was sleeping it off. Well, he'd fixed her. Real good. Another time the lousy cop bastards threw his ass in jail.

Five thousand. Man! Like a Christmas present. Almost Christmas, wasn't it? Yeah, the best Christmas present he'd ever had. Only present in so long he couldn't remember the last one. Five large. Oh, baby, all the things he could do with that much green. Good booze, better than Jack, hundred-and-one-proof Wild Turkey. And some young meat. Maybe a kid like in Pablo's pictures, he'd never had one of them. All the things. Five large. Just thinking about his Christmas present put a glow in him like two of three slugs of sour mash, took away some of the cold.

Time yet? Almost. Few more minutes. He didn't have no watch, but he didn't need no watch. Never had, never would. He had this thing in him, this what-youcallit . . . internal clock. Yeah. Always knew what time it was, down to within five-ten minutes of clock time. Born with it inside, nobody could figure it out. A fuggin' medical marvel, that was him. Nobody'd believed it, he'd lay bets and collect every time. That one time, when he was in the navy and those five gobs bet him ten bucks each they could shut him up in a dark room and leave him there and when they let him out again he couldn't tell them how long he'd been locked up, what time it was. He showed them bastards, all right. Told 'em how long, told 'em what time it was within five minutes. They paid up, too. He made sure they paid up. Another of his lucky times. Only that one hadn't lasted neither because some son of a bitch swiped the fifty while he was asleep. One of them five sailors, sure, but he couldn't never find out which one it was.

Shit, the things you remember. Good luck, bad luck, one or the other his whole fuggin' life. Hell of a lot more bad than good until he followed that crazy Spook and found his stash. Pretty good for a week, crappy yesterday, good again tonight. Good for good, this time. Five large. Oh, man, good for *good!*

He sat there thinking about the money, warming himself on it, planning all the things he was gonna do with that cash. Wasn't too long before that old internal clock went off. Time to meet the man. Time to meet the five thousand in person. Hello, baby. Hello, you big green Christmas present, come to papa.

Up on his feet. He worked some of the kinks out, limbered up his bones, before he went over and cracked the door. Rain had let up a little. More good luck. He eased out. Nobody in the alley. He squeezed through the peel in the fence, walked careful toward Army Street. Two blocks to the park down there. Didn't see no cops on the way. Yeah, his luck had turned good for sure.

He set up in a doorway across from the park, right where he had the last time. And here come the car, right on time. Pulled over to the curb and the man leaned over to shove the door open.

"Get in," he said.

"Nah. Just gimme my Christmas present."

"Your what?"

"My money. Gimme my five large."

"Not here. Get in."

"You give it to me here last time."

"There's a lot more this time. And it's in the trunk. Come on, come on, I saw a couple of patrol cars when I came off the freeway. You want to risk getting picked up? I sure as hell don't."

Big old car's heater was on. Big Dog could feel the warm air coming out at him, and the cold wind shoving at his back. He got into the car. Yeah, real warm in there. Felt good on his face, his hands.

Man said shut the door and he shut it. Car jumped ahead, out onto Army. Slid into a U-turn next block, come back toward the freeway.

"Where we goin'?"

"Someplace private, safe."

"You better have my fuggin' money."

"I've got it."

"Better have, man. Told you I got everything wrote down, buddy takes it straight to the cops if I don't come back with the cash."

"Don't worry. What happens after you get it?"

"Told you that too. You never hear from me no more."

"That's what you said when we paid you the five hundred."

"Yeah, well, I mean it this time."

"Sure you do."

"I'm splittin' from Frisco. Goin' where it's warm."

"Tonight?"

"Maybe. Yeah, maybe tonight."

"Bus? You want a ride to the bus depot after we're done?"

"Nah. You just bring me back where you picked me up."

They were on the freeway now. Big Dog settled back, stretched his feet close to the heater vents. Nice and warm in here, gonna be nice and warm in Dago. Goin' back in style. He grinned to himself. And when the five thousand was gone he'd hit the man up for another five. And another five and another after that. This here Sandy Claus knew what was good for him, he'd keep his bag full of presents for the Big Dog.

On a freeway exit now. He leaned his head up, blinking. Dark street, looked like some kind of industrial area.

"Almost there," Sandy Claus said.

"Where? Where we at?"

"Where you get paid off."

Sharp left turn. Big old warehouse, no lights, asphalt lot behind it all dark and wet. Car stopped, headlights went down dim.

"All right, get out."

"What for?"

"You want what's coming to you, don't you?"

"You go get it, man. Warm in here, cold outside."

"Get out of the car."

Different voice, all hot and pissed. Big Dog looked at him. Then his mouth dropped open and he sat up all the way, staring. The man had a gun in his hand, a goddamn big mother pistol.

"Hey," he said, "hey, what's the idea?"

"The idea is you get out like I told you to."

"Nah. You can't —"

"Get out of the car! Or I swear I'll blow your head off right where you sit!"

Big Dog felt sick all of a sudden, couldn't think straight no more. He got out. Rain and cold again. Bad luck again. Shit, he never did have no good luck that lasted. Just jerking himself around, thinking he had. Always turned bad, like he was cursed or something. He wished to Christ he had a drink. He needed one worse than ever.

The man come around behind the car, stood a few feet away from him. Taillights lit him up all red, him and his gun. Red glow, black gun, black shadows.

"You can't do nothin' to me," Big Dog said. "I got it all wrote down. I give it to a buddy of mine —"

"You don't have any buddies. Not garbage like you."

"I got it all wrote down —"

"Bullshit. I don't believe you. Even if I did, it doesn't matter anymore. I've had all I can take, I can't swallow anymore. All you bloodsuckers, all you garbage, squeezing a man, hurting people I care about, ruining their lives, ruining my life. Grinding me down, trampling me. I took it all these years but no more, no more. Now it's my turn."

"You're fuggin' crazy."

"If I am, it's bastards like you made me that way. I don't care. I don't care what happens anymore."

Big Dog didn't care no more neither. He felt sick, he couldn't think straight, he needed a drink bad. And he was starting to get pissed off himself. His head hurt like somebody was sticking it with nails and wires. Fug this guy. Fug him! He started forward.

"That's it," the guy said, "that's right, come and get your Christmas present."

Big Dog kept on moving, but not for long. "Christmas present" was the last thing he ever heard.

16

Kerry said, "The pier looks nice this year. Really festive."

"Yeah," I said. "Festive."

"Look at all the displays, how inventive they are."

I looked. "At least they don't have some poor schnook dressed up in a Santa Claus suit."

"I suppose that's a reference to the Gala Christmas Benefit. You're never going to let me forget that, are you?"

"Ho, ho, ho."

She poked me in the ribs. "Don't be grumpy."

"I'm not grumpy."

"If you're going to be grumpy . . ."

I said again, grumpily, that I wasn't grumpy. It was the truth, more or less. Ill at ease was the proper term. She knew how large parties affected me; we'd been together long enough for her to know me inside out. Why call me grumpy?

The crowd was much larger, it seemed to me, than the last Season of Sharing party I'd attended. The huge open space where Pier 24-½'s inhabitants usually parked their cars was packed with milling, chattering, laughing, bibulous, face-stuffing humanity: grouped thickly around a buffet table and bar toward the far end; swirling around the decorative displays, the pedestaled loving cup that would be awarded to the best display at the close of festivities, the red, white and blue donation barrels spotted here and there. The raising of funds and goods for charity was the point of these gatherings — a different charity each year, with one of the pier's firms handling the collection and disbursement on a rotating basis. The party atmosphere may have left me cold, but I was all for its purpose. I even had a certain personal involvement in this year's cause, because of the Spook investigation. Ted Smalley had told me that a group called Home for the Holidays, dedicated to housing and feeding the homeless during the season, would be the current recipient.

Kerry prodded me into the midst of the noisy throng. I had to admit that the displays were pretty clever, all right. McCone

Investigations' offices were off the upstairs catwalk to the left; garlands were woven all along the railing in front and a lot of silver stars, moons, planets, and crystal beads hung down from them. The architects on the opposite catwalk, Chandler & Santos, had fashioned a cityscape of colored lights and neon tubing; their neighbors, a group of CPAs, had suspended cardboard cutouts of people of all races holding hands. Down here I saw a couple that Emily might have liked: a miniature Santa's Village, complete with electric tram, courtesy of the firm of marketing consultants; and a forest of small fir trees dusted in realistic-looking snow, where replicas of various endangered animals seemed to be hiding (ecological nonprofit outfit). There was also a Model T Ford with a life-size St. Nick at the wheel and presents in the rumbleseat (car leasing agency). One of these would win the loving cup and pier bragging rights for the coming year.

We wove and squeezed our way past some of the patriotic barrels, all of which were already stuffed full of canned goods, new toys, and warm clothing, and stopped in front of another, smaller barrel on a low wooden platform. Propped up there was a big sign:

HOME FOR THE HOLIDAYS
Season of Sharing Fund
Be generous!

Kerry transferred a folded twenty-dollar bill from her purse into the barrel. I took a ten out of my wallet.

"For heaven's sake," she said, "don't be a Scrooge. Read the sign."

I said, "Be generous, Mr. Spade."

"What's that?"

"Never mind." I exchanged the ten for two twenties, stepped up to the platform and slotted them into the barrel.

"That's better. Oh, here's Sharon."

McCone came bustling up, as svelte and attractive as ever despite the furred Santa Claus cap she wore over her black hair. Just looking at the cap made my scalp itch. She hugged Kerry, waved some green plant-stuff over my head, and then kissed me on the mouth.

"Hey," I said, "I'm a married man. And you're almost young enough to be my daughter."

"Almost?"

"Don't mind him," Kerry said. "He's in one of his grumpy moods."

"I am not grumpy!"

McCone said, "Well, whatever you are,

Wolf, I'm glad you're here." She knew I didn't care for that pet name — short for "lone wolf detective," an allusion to the hardboiled pulp sleuths — which was probably one of the reasons she insisted on using it. Her sense of humor is a little bent and barbed, not unlike Kerry's. "We were afraid you'd try to cancel out at the last minute."

"No way that was going to happen," Kerry said.

"Is Tamara coming?"

I shook my head. "Not in a party mood, she said."

"The split with her boyfriend?"

"Right. Worse time of year for something like that."

"There's never a good time. She going to be okay?"

"I hope so. Where's Ripinsky?"

"He had to fly down to RKI headquarters in San Diego. Urgent business." Hy Ripinsky was a fellow investigator specializing in high-profile international hostage negotiation, and her significant other. "But he'll be back in time for us to spend Christmas and New Year's together."

She and Kerry proceeded to jabber about the party, the displays in general and something called "the galactic theme" in

213

particular, the fund-raising goal of five thousand cash for the homeless. It never ceases to amaze me how adaptable women are. Put two together, even a pair of strangers, in any social situation and not only are they immediately comfortable with each other and their surroundings, they never seem at a loss for words.

While they were chattering, I glanced around some more. What galactic theme? I thought.

Pretty soon Kerry paused long enough to suggest I go and fetch drinks. "White wine for me," she said. "Sharon?"

"The same."

So I waded alone through the sea of partygoers to the bar. The noise level in the cavernous space, enhanced by a loud-speakered version of "Deck the Halls," was such that I had to raise my voice to a near-shout to place my order. Two white wines, nothing for me. My brain gets fuzzy enough at parties as it is.

Somebody came up and tapped my arm while I was waiting. Ted Smalley. His bookseller partner, Neal Osborn, was beside him. Both wore red stocking caps with tassels and somehow managed not to look ridiculous.

Neal said, "Nice party, isn't it? Didn't

Ted do a terrific job coordinating the displays?"

"Terrific," I said. "Great, uh, galactic theme, Ted."

He beamed at me. "Everyone cooperated, for a change."

Neal ordered for the two of them. Then he said to Ted, "Shall we spring it on him now or wait until later?"

"Now. I can't wait to see his face."

"Why don't you do the honors?"

"No, you go ahead."

"No, it was your idea."

"Well, mine and Sharon's."

I said, "What're you two talking about?"

"You'll find out," Neal said. "It's waiting for you upstairs in Sharon's office, on her desk."

"What is?"

"Look for Christmas wrap and a big bow."

"A present? Why would you get me a present?"

"For your help on the Patterson case," Ted said.

"You've already paid me for that."

"A present isn't payment." He pressed a key into my hand. "Spare key to her office. It's locked."

I didn't know what to say except "I don't

know what to say." I'm not used to gifts from anyone other than Kerry and, the past three years, Tamara. This Christmas, there'd be one from Emily too. And now McCone Investigations.

"Don't open it up there," Ted said. "Bring it down so we can all watch."

Oh, dandy. Being the center of a ring of eyes is something else that makes me sweat.

I delivered the glasses of wine, told Kerry where I was going — Sharon grinned when I mentioned the present — and then made my way upstairs. As I approached McCone's private office, I had the spare key ready. But I didn't need it. The door was closed but not locked.

No cause for suspicion in that, but what I saw when I opened the door and walked in set off alarm bells in my head. A man had been hunched over her desk — a blond man who didn't work for McCone Investigations. He wheeled, straightening, and flashed me a frightened-deer look. He seemed to teeter briefly on the edge of panic, then with an effort he got a grip on himself and pasted on a weak smile. He was familiar; I'd seen him around the pier before. An employee of one of the other firms . . . the architects on the opposite catwalk. His name was Kennett or Bennett.

"You startled me," he said. "What're you doing here?"

"I'll ask you the same question."

"Sharon asked me to get something for her. If you'll excuse me . . ."

He edged past where I stood, not making eye contact, one hand squeezed into the pocket of a pair of tight leather pants. In other circumstances, or if he'd lingered a few more seconds, I would have acted to restrain him; as it was I hesitated long enough for him to get past me and out the door.

I followed as he hurried along the cat-walk, close to the garland-festooned railing, his hand still in his pocket. He glanced back once, saw me coming and seemed to quicken his pace even more. Only fifty feet separated us when he reached the stairs. I had a clear look at him all the way to the bottom, but as I started down, the Model T Ford display cut off my view and the party swirl swallowed him.

I ran down steps until most of the pier floor was visible again. No more than fifteen seconds ticked off before I spotted him again. He'd stopped and joined a small group near the loving cup, was now making a gesture with the hand that had been in his pocket. The hand appeared to be empty. And McCone was not one of the group.

Another few seconds and I had her located. She was with Ted and one of her operatives, a former FBI agent named Craig Morland. I went straight to her, keeping my eye on Leather Pants all the way.

"Did you send somebody up to your office a few minutes ago?" I asked her. "Somebody besides me who doesn't work for you?"

Frown. "No. Why?"

I told her why. "Five-ten or so, blond hair, dressed in black leather pants and a thin-ribbed sweater. I think he works for the architects. Bennett, Kennett?"

"Paul Kennett. He's a draftsman for Chandler & Santos. My office door was locked — how'd he get in?"

"I don't know, but it wasn't locked when I got there."

"What was he doing?"

"Couldn't tell," I said, "but he was at your desk. Claimed you'd sent him to get something for you, but he had a guilty, scared look. He got past me before I thought to stop him and hustled down here. He's over by the trophy now, talking to some people, pretending nothing happened."

McCone said, "That's damn funny. Now that I think about it, he's been hanging around the offices all week. I practically tripped over him once."

"In Julia's and my office almost every day," Morland said, "trying to put the moves on her. Wouldn't take no for an answer, just kept coming back."

"Suspicious. He's never bothered her like that before, has he?"

"No."

"I don't like him," Ted put in. "Big ego and an attitude to match."

"We'll find out what this is all about. Craig, keep an eye on him. Make sure he doesn't leave the pier."

"Right."

"Ted, find Julia, Mick and Charlotte. Just in case we need them."

The two men moved off. Sharon turned to me. "Let's go upstairs, see what Kennett might've been after."

"Any ideas?"

"Yes, and I hope I'm wrong."

The blare of one of those stupid novelty songs, "Grandma Got Run Over by a Reindeer," followed us up to the catwalk. I'd shut but not paused to lock the door to

McCone's office; we pushed inside. At her desk, she began pawing through the pile of stuff in her In-box.

"Dammit! It's gone."

"What is?"

"Computer disk. My final report on the Patterson case."

"Oh, brother."

"There're all sorts of specific evidentiary references on that disk. If Patterson gets hold of it, he'll know exactly what we've got. He might be able to cover up enough to keep the D.A. from convicting him and his cronies, maybe enough to forestall indictments."

"How'd Kennett know about the disk? What's his connection to the case?"

She didn't answer. Something on the floor alongside her desk had caught her eye. She bent to scoop it up, looked at it and then held it out to me. Key. Shiny new, as if it had been recently cut. She compared it to her own office key. Exact duplicate.

"Now I'm sure Kennett's responsible," she said. "I run a pretty open shop here; you know that. The same key operates all the doors so staff members will have access to the other offices if they need something. We trust each other, so we tend to trust the other pier tenants too. Made it simple for Kennett to snag a key while he was hanging around Julia and have a copy made. This isn't the first time he's used it, either, I'll bet."

"No?"

"Yesterday morning our creaky old office safe was open when I came in. I thought one of the staff must've left it that way, even though none of them owned up to it."

"Anything taken?"

"Nothing. There's not much in it except petty cash and my .357 Magnum, but they weren't disturbed."

"Kennett looking for the disk."

"Yes. And I should've been more careful."

I asked again, "What's his connection to the case?"

"All I can do right now is guess," McCone said. "He must know Patterson or one of the others involved. Architects and city planners all know one another. Somebody found out we were conducting an investigation — a leak somewhere, or a trail we didn't sweep clean — and paid or coerced Kennett into finding out what we knew. As often as he was in and out of the offices the past week, he could have overheard one of us mention the disk."

I said, "He was only out of my sight for a few seconds. It's either still on him or somewhere close by."

"Wherever it is, we'd damn well better find it. If we don't, there goes weeks of work, a fat fee, and my hard-earned professional reputation."

17

From the catwalk we located Kennett, drink in hand, wandering casually through the crowd. By the time we got to the pier floor he'd stopped by the Santa's Village display, was standing there by himself looking at it. When he saw us, the grim look on McCone's face, it was like watching somebody put on a mask. Blank, smiling innocence, the kind Nixon used to project in front of TV cameras.

Sharon said, "Where's the disk?"

"What disk?"

"The one you stole from my private office."

"Stole? I don't know what you're talking about."

"Do you deny you were in my office a few minutes ago?"

"I certainly do. I haven't been anywhere near your office."

I said, "We both know that's a lie, Kennett."

"Who're you? I don't know you."

"You're not leaving here with that disk," McCone said.

"I don't have any damn disk." Bluster now, but with an undercurrent of fear. He gulped what was left in his plastic cup, set the cup on the floor, and then extended his arms dramatically. In a loud voice he said, "Search me if you want to. Go ahead, search me!"

People in the vicinity stopped talking, turned to stare — just what he wanted. Neither Sharon nor I moved. There was no point in searching him, we both knew that. His leather pants were skin tight; the outline of a disk would have shown clearly. Same thing with the ribbed pullover. A computer disk might fit inside one of the loafers he was wearing, but he hadn't had time to stuff it in there; and even if he had, it would probably have changed the way he walked. He didn't have it on him. He'd gotten rid of it somewhere, and not very long after he left McCone's office.

"All right, Kennett. You win this round." She jabbed him on the chest with a sharp-nailed forefinger, as hard as I would have. "But we'll find it if it takes all night. You'll be under watch until we do."

"If you try to hold me against my will,

224

I'll sue you. You and this man and any-body else involved. Don't think I won't."

More bluster. Neither of us bothered to respond.

Sharon McCone is as efficient an investi-gator as I've known in thirty-some years in the business. Doubly so in a crisis. She gathered and quickly briefed the members of her staff, individually and in pairs, telling Craig Morland to stay close to Ken-nett everywhere he went, assigning her nephew, Mick, and her newest operative, Julia Rafael, to watch the exits. The rest of us went upstairs to her office, Neal Osborn and Kerry included. Neal because we might need an extra hand, Kerry because she'd noticed Kennett hurrying downstairs with me in his wake.

Once we were all settled, Sharon behind her desk, the rest of us sitting or standing, she said, "We need to brainstorm this, try to get some idea of what Kennett did with the disk. Wolf and I will do most of the talking, but if anybody has anything to contribute, jump in any time." That was another thing about McCone: She ran a fairly loose ship, delegating a good deal of authority to her people, but when she took command she did it forcefully and got complete cooperation in return. In my idealized view of the future, Tamara would turn out just like her. You couldn't ask for a better role model.

She asked me to go over again, in detail, what had happened earlier. When I was done, she said, "So Kennett didn't go around to the opposite catwalk before he went downstairs, and Craig said he hasn't gone up there since. That eliminates the Chandler & Santos offices as a hiding place."

"We can eliminate one other possibility," I said. "The unlikely one that Kennett hid the disk somewhere in here *before* I walked in. The old purloined letter trick. He didn't expect to get caught and he'd be a fool to risk sneaking in another time, or trying to retrieve it while you were here."

She nodded. "You had him in sight the whole time after he left, except for those few seconds on your way downstairs?"

"Right."

"How many seconds, would you say?"

"No more than fifteen. That little window must be when he got rid of the disk."

"Unless he managed to hide it on the way. Up here among the railing decorations, for instance."

"I doubt it, but I can't be a hundred percent certain. He did walk close to the railing all the way to the stairs. It's remotely possible he slipped the disk in among the decorations."

"The main argument against it is the same as hiding it in here — he couldn't've been sure of getting his hands on it later. All the decorations between here and the stairs are ours. Still . . . Ted, go check and make sure."

As Ted went out, I said, "Kennett had one hand in his pocket on the catwalk, on the stairs, and when I lost sight of him. But when I spotted him again, the hand was out — he made a gesture with it when he joined the group by the trophy. It's possible that he passed the disk to somebody in the crowd."

"Not likely. He'd've had no reason to arrange for an accomplice. It feels like a one-man operation to me."

"Which leaves a hiding place someplace on the pier floor."

"Did he turn straight into the crowd from the stairs?"

"Yes. Hard left turn."

"So he passed right by the Model T Ford display."

"Right, because that was what cut off my view of him."

Charlotte Keim, Mick's girlfriend and fellow computer whiz, said, "Another possibility is the nonprofit's ecological display. It's right next to the car."

McCone said, "Among the branches of one of the fir trees? Could be."

"The only problem with that is, he'd've had to go right in among them. That'd be inviting attention."

"Have a look anyway, Charlotte. As unobtrusively as possible."

Ted came in just then, shaking his head. "It's not among the garlands or galactic decorations."

"Check the Model T next. Inside and out."

Neal said, "I'll help him look."

The three of them left together. Sharon asked Kerry, "You also lost sight of Kennett for several seconds, you said?"

"Yes. About the same number, fifteen."

"Where was he when you spotted him again?"

"By Santa's Village, on his way toward the loving cup."

"The way the village is constructed, it'd be hard to hide anything in it quickly, even an object as small as a computer disk."

"What about the cup?" Kerry asked. "If it's hollow, he could have dropped it inside."

"It's hollow, but Kennett isn't very tall and the way the cup sits on the pedestal, he'd've had to stretch up on his toes. Again, too conspicuous."

I said, "Then it has to be either the Model T or the fir trees."

Wrong. It was neither one. First Charlotte, then Ted and Neal returned empty-handed. Neal said, "I even got down on my hands and knees and checked the undercarriage. You should've seen the looks I got."

We all lapsed into a period of ruminative silence. Frustration had thickened the tension in the room, increased the sense of urgency. Sharon usually maintains a poker face in business situations, tense or otherwise, but the worry was beginning to show through. She had a lot riding on the recovery of that disk.

I broke the silence finally by saying, "We've been assuming that if I hadn't come in unexpectedly and caught Kennett in the act, he would've hung onto the disk until the party ended. But remember how he's dressed. If he'd kept it in his pocket, as tight as those leather pants are, he'd have to keep his hand in there too so it wouldn't show."

"You're right," McCone said. "That would really call attention to himself, the last thing he'd want. If he'd intended to hold onto the disk, he'd've worn looser clothing."

"So he must've planned to hide it all along. Someplace picked out in advance, one he'd be sure to have access to later. Easy access, when nobody was around."

"Yes, but what place? What've we overlooked?"

"Kerry, when you saw him passing Santa's Village, was he moving straight toward the trophy?"

". . . No, he wasn't. At an angle, a sharp one."

"From which direction?"

"The right."

"Then he had to have veered off from the Model T display, toward the center of the floor, then veered back again."

"That's right."

"Aimless wandering, maybe. And maybe not. The bar and the buffet are in the center, but farther back. What's closer to this end?"

"Nothing, except — Oh! Of course."

The rest of us got it at the same time.

Mick said, "Home for the Holidays."

I said, "And the sign says 'Be generous.' "

Ted said, "And this year it's Chandler and Santos's turn to disperse the donations."

McCone said, "That's it, that's got to be where he put the disk."

Paul Kennett's unfunny private joke, his own personal donation to the homeless: he'd dropped it right through that little slot into the Season of Sharing Fund barrel as he passed by.

We waited until the end of the party to check the barrel and confront Kennett. The Patterson case was sensitive, and more than one of the guests had political or media connections; and there was no point in spoiling the festivities for everyone else. McCone sent Ted and Neal downstairs to brief Craig, Mick, and Julia, and to stand guard over the cash barrel. The rest of us sat in her office, nibbled food that Ted had sent up, and talked about this and that. I'm not a patient man, normally, but tonight I had no trouble with fidgeting or clock-watching. Sharon's quiet, comfortable office was a far better place for me than down among the noisy revelers on the pier floor.

At a few minutes past eleven, Neal poked his head through the door. "The pier's locked down and the clean-up crews are assembling."

We all trooped down into a wasteland of party wreckage. The decorations, fresh and colorful when Kerry and I arrived, now looked as tired as the people from the pier offices who had volunteered to remain and clean up the mess. McCone pointed out the two partners in the architectural firm, Nat Chandler and Harvey Santos, who were hauling one of the barrels of clothing up the stairs to their offices. Paul Kennett was nowhere to be seen.

Mick was leaning casually on the cash barrel, talking to Ted. Sharon said to him, "You're supposed to be watching the back entrance."

"No need. Kennett went upstairs about ten minutes ago. Probably waiting in his office for the money barrel to be brought up. What do you bet he volunteered to stay and count the cash after everybody else goes home?"

Santos and Chandler were coming back down. McCone signaled to them, said when they came over that she wanted them to act as witnesses, and then nodded to Mick and me.

We pried the lid off the barrel. It was three-quarters full of cash, coins, checks. We tilted it at a forty-five degree angle, and I held it like that so Mick could root around inside. It wasn't much more than a minute before he came up with a flat, round object encased in a thin plastic sleeve.

One of the architects asked Sharon, "A computer disk? What's this about?" She didn't answer; she was looking up at the catwalk in front of their offices.

Paul Kennett stood at the railing, staring down at us. She took the disk from Mick's hand, held it high over her head. Kennett had nowhere to go; he didn't try. Not even when Mick said loud enough for him to hear, "Gotcha!"

Later, most of us reassembled in McCone's office for some Christmas cheer. The disk was safe for tonight; tomorrow she would have copies made and lock them in her safe deposit box, along with the hard-copy evidence files, until it was time for her Monday meeting with the D.A. As for Kennett, he'd avoided arrest and prosecution for theft because of the need to avoid publicity; but he'd been warned to keep his mouth shut if he didn't want to be named in the forthcoming indictment against Patterson. What he hadn't avoided was the loss of his job. Chandler and Santos had summarily fired him as soon as they were made aware of what he'd done.

I'd forgotten all about my Christmas present, which Sharon had slipped into a desk drawer during our earlier session. But she hadn't forgotten. As soon as we were settled with our drinks, she produced the package and handed it to me with a little flourish.

"With thanks and love from all of us," she said.

Embarrassed, I said, "I haven't gotten anything for any of you yet . . ."

"Never mind that. Open your gift, Wolf."

I hefted it. Not very large, not very heavy. I stripped off the paper, removed the lid from an oblong box — and inside was another, smaller box sealed with a lot of Scotch tape. Ted's doing; I could tell from his expression. So I used my pocket knife to slice through the tape, opened the second box, rifled through a wad of tissue paper, and found —

Two plastic-bagged issues of *Black Mask*. And not just any two issues: rare, fine-condition copies of the September 1929 and February 1930 numbers, each containing an installment of the original six-part serial version of Hammett's *The Maltese Falcon*.

My mouth was hanging open; I snapped it shut. When I looked up they were all grinning at me. I said, "How'd you know these were the only two *Falcon* issues I didn't have?" Funny, but my voice sounded a little choked.

"I told them," Kerry said. "I checked to make sure."

"And one of my book contacts back east found the issues," Neal said.

"They must've cost a small fortune. So scarce and expensive I didn't even put them on the want list I gave you . . ."

McCone waved that away. "What they cost doesn't matter. You've been a friend for a long time. It's the season of sharing with friends, too."

I just sat there.

Kerry said, "Aren't you going to say something?"

Sure, right. But what can you say to friends and loved ones who treat you better than you deserve, that doesn't sound woefully inadequate?

18

Jake Runyon

Joshua was late. No surprise there. Wouldn't be a surprise if he didn't show at all.

The restaurant was off 18th Street, on the fringe of the predominantly gay Castro district. Noisy, dark, crowded. Joshua's choice; his brief message on the answering machine had given the name and address of the place and the time, Saturday noon. Nearly all of the customers were male and some had inventoried Runyon when he came in, cataloged and dismissed him. He looked like what he was — straight, and a member of the law enforcement establishment — and they didn't want anything to do with him. He'd been ignored ever since, except by a waiter who looked elsewhere while he quickly unloaded a menu and a glass of water.

Runyon sat waiting with his hands palms-up on the table. When he thought about anything, it was the Spook case. He hadn't found Big Dog last night; and as of this morning, the authorities hadn't picked him up yet either. Buried somewhere, but not deep enough. Wouldn't matter to the agency's investigation whether he got flushed out and chained or not, as long as the identity question could be answered in Mono County. He'd done his part, would keep on hunting if Big Dog was still at large when he got back, but the extra effort was for himself, not for the agency or the law or to see justice done. He'd quit believing in justice, man's and God's both, when he was told Colleen's cancer was terminal.

Mostly, sitting alone in the noisy restaurant, he kept his mind cranked down to basic awareness. There'd been a time when he was not good at waiting, but that was long ago and far away. He'd learned. His years as a cop and a private investigator, all the stakeouts and travel time and downtime reports, had been partly responsible. But it hadn't been until the past few months that he'd really learned how to do it. In doctors' offices and hospital lobbies, at home during all the sleepless nights with the phone close beside him. Nothing taught you patience, the art of shutting yourself down for extended periods of time, like waiting for someone you loved to leave you forever.

He'd been there nearly half an hour when his son finally showed. He knew how long it had been because he was facing the entrance and when Joshua walked in, he glanced automatically at his watch. Joshua scanned the room; then his shoulders squared and he approached in measured steps. His whole demeanor said: Get it over with.

His mouth said, "Are you Jake Runyon?" in the same cold, formal tone he'd used on the phone.

"You know I am. Sit down, son."

"I wasn't sure you'd still be here."

"Why not? You're not that late."

"I almost didn't come at all."

"What you almost didn't do isn't important."

Joshua sat down. They studied each other, like stray dogs coming together for the first time — a kind of sniffing and keening. His mother's eyes, all right. Bright, smoky blue, and raddled with emotion. Discomfort: he didn't seem to know where to put his hands. Hostility, defiance: his unblinking stare was a challenge. Righteousness: he was dealing with somebody he'd been told all his life was evil.

The waiter appeared. Joshua said without shifting his gaze, "I don't want anything."

Runyon said, "Grilled cheese sandwich and tea, any kind."

"Tea? I thought people like you drank beer or whiskey for lunch."

"You sure you don't want to eat?"

"I'm not hungry."

The waiter went away. Joshua shifted position, hid his hands in his lap. He said, "I suppose you've been wondering why I picked this place."

"Not really. You don't live far away."

"You know what this neighborhood is, don't you?"

"I've got eyes."

"That's why I live here." Harsh, confrontational: "I'm gay."

Runyon was silent.

"You understand? Gay, homosexual. Your only child is a fag."

Silent.

"Well? Aren't you going to say anything?"

"What do you expect me to say?"

"Don't tell me you're not shocked."

"I'm not."

"You already knew, is that it?"

"I didn't know. Until you just told me."

"Suspected it, then."

"I never gave it any thought."

"For God's sake, you don't even act surprised."

"I suppose I am, a little."

"Disappointed? Angry? Disgusted?"

"None of the above," Runyon said. "Your sexual orientation isn't important to me. None of my business."

Joshua seemed nonplussed; it wasn't the reaction he'd anticipated, prepared for, and it seemed to have pitched him partway off his high horse. In less harsh tones he said, "Just what is important to you?"

"Where you're concerned? That you're happy, healthy, secure."

"Oh, come off it."

"You asked, I told you."

"Well, I don't have AIDS yet. Does that make you feel better?"

"What would make me feel better is less hostility and more civility."

"Civility, no less. Such a big word."

"There's not enough in the world. Not enough of a lot of things — honesty, integrity, compassion, understanding."

"Christ. Liberal sentiments from a cop."

"Not all law officers are fascist homophobes, you know. Besides, I'm not a cop any longer."

"Private eye. Same damn thing."

"No it isn't. You don't know my profession."

"I don't care about your profession."

"You don't know me, I don't know you. That's why we're here."

"Establish a father-son bond?" Joshua said bitterly. "It's about twenty years too late for that."

"Not too late for you to hear my side of the story."

"I don't want to hear any of your lies."

"I told you on the phone, I don't lie."

"I've known liars who said the same thing. Dammit, why couldn't you have stayed in Seattle? Why did you have to move down here?"

"You know the answer to that," Runyon said. "You're all I have left now."

"And I told you, you *don't* have me, any part of me. You may be my biological father, but that's all you are or ever will be. Why can't you get it through your head that I don't want anything to do with you?"

"I understand it, all right. I understand the reasons too."

"After what you did to my mother —"

"It's what she did to herself and to you that you don't understand yet."

"She didn't do anything to me except love me and raise me! Alone! After you abandoned us for that bitch —"

Runyon caught Joshua's wrist and pinned it hard against the table, fingers digging like metal into the flesh, bringing a grimace and a low cry of pain. He leaned forward. "Let's get one thing straight right now. Say or think anything you want about me, but if I hear you call Colleen any more names or slander her memory in any way, I'll knock you down and step on your face. Understood?"

"For God's sake —"

"I'm not kidding. Understood?"

"Yes. All right, yes." Runyon let go of him. There were angry red marks on the wrist; Joshua massaged them gingerly, avoiding eye contact. "I . . . I'm sorry."

Runyon gestured that away. "Don't say what you don't mean."

"I won't mention her again. But I won't listen to anything ugly from you about my mother, either."

"No name-calling or mudslinging, that was never my intention. But sometimes the truth is ugly."

"Here we go again. The last honest man."

"I meant what I said. I won't lie to you."

"You're not going to change my mind about anything. I know what happened between you and my mother."

"You know what she told you. Her version. I'm a monster, she was a helpless victim."

"Well?"

"There're some things I'll bet she left out."

"Such as?"

"That I was in touch with a lawyer before I met Colleen, to start divorce proceedings and to try to get custody of you. Didn't know that, did you?"

". . . That's crap."

"I'll give you the lawyer's name. He's still practicing in Seattle."

"Some friend of yours who'd say anything . . ."

"Her post-partum depression, the episode in the bathtub — she ever talk about that?"

Uncertainty seeped in to mix with Joshua's disbelief. "What're you talking about? What episode?"

"Severe post-partum depression that led to heavy drinking and neglect of your care. I came home early one afternoon and found her in the tub, passed out drunk, holding you in her arms. You were asleep but your head was barely above water. If she'd slipped down any farther, you'd've drowned."

"Liar! That's a fucking lie!"

"I'll say it again — I don't lie."

"She wasn't like that, she —"

"I'll give you the name of the doctor who treated her. Or maybe you think a doctor would falsify his records as a favor to somebody he hasn't seen in twenty years?"

"I don't . . . it wasn't until she found about you and . . . she didn't start drinking until after you abandoned us . . ."

"She started drinking at sixteen," Runyon said, "and she never stopped. She drank before we were married, before and after you were born. Her father and mother were both alcoholics — her father died of it, same as she did. I can document that, too, if you want me to. She needed booze to unwind, to be happy, to make love, to get through the day. You lived with her nearly two decades, you're not blind or stupid. You know I'm telling the truth."

The cords in Joshua's neck showed as sharply as ax blades. "I *don't* know it. You're trying to trash her memory the way you trashed her life!"

244

"You couldn't be more wrong. I loved your mother in the beginning —"

"Bullshit!"

"— but I couldn't live with her any more."

"Couldn't live with *me* anymore."

"I told you, I tried to get custody —"

"If that's so . . . God knows what my life would be like now if you'd succeeded. What *I'd* be like."

"Not so bitter, maybe. Not so filled with hate."

"The only person I hate is you."

"That's what I mean," Runyon said. "Look, I know she loved you and you loved her. I know she raised you alone, did the best job she could. I just want you to see her as she really was."

"Sick, selfish, spiteful?"

"And self-destructive. Flawed human being, not a blameless saint —"

"That's enough!" Joshua shoved his chair back, stood up so fast it clattered against the empty table behind him. "I won't listen to any more of this!"

Runyon watched him stomp away blindly, almost colliding with one of the waiters. The entrance door cracked like a pistol shot behind him. Some of the customers were staring at Runyon, dislike on the faces of those close enough to have overheard. One of them said loudly to another, "Poor bugger. An asshole for a father, just like mine."

Runyon ignored him. He sat the way he had before his son's arrival, stiff-backed, hands palms-up on the table. He was still sitting that way when the waiter brought his sandwich and tea, set the plate and cup down harder than necessary. Runyon ignored him, too.

It had gone badly, but then he'd expected it would. Colleen would've known how to handle a situation like this; she'd been tactful, seemed always to have the right words at her command. But he was a blunt man, and his way was to plow ahead doing and saying what he believed had to be done and said. Joshua needed to hear the truth, no matter how much it hurt him or added fuel to his hatred. For his own good, even if it ended any chance of a reconciliation between them. He'd never really believed that would happen anyway. Hard enough fighting through twenty years' worth of Andrea's lies, half-truths, and self-serving omissions to try to forge a simple understanding.

He had no appetite, but he ate his sandwich and drank his tea. Colleen had never liked it when he or anyone else wasted food.

It was snowing in the Sierras. Just a light dusting on the way up Highway 80 to Donner summit, and the highway was clear; but there had been heavier falls recently — the snowplowed drifts along the verges proved that — and the Chains Required signs were liable to come out before he got all the way across. He had a set of chains in the Ford; you needed chains often enough during Washington state winters. But it was a hassle putting them on and taking them off, and driving with chains made him edgy at the best of times. Long, uninterrupted drives allowed him to relax, to shut down to basic awareness.

He made it across the summit at slow-down speed but without having to stop. There wasn't much snow at the lower elevations, and none at all in Reno or Carson City or points south on Highway 395. It started coming down again at nightfall, near Topaz Lake on the Nevada/California border, and stayed with him across into Mono County and most of the way to Sonora Junction. Heavy enough to cover the road and retard speed, but this was high desert country, flanked by the massive

Sierras on the west and smaller mountain ranges on the east; through here it was flat enough to make chains unnecessary. Still, the snowfall required sharp attention, tightened his shoulder and back muscles, put a tired grit into his eyes.

Nearly 8:30 when he reached Aspen Creek. He could tell little about it in the darkness, other than it was small and its main drag had been plowed recently; the low drifts along the roadway were smooth and even, gleaming pure white in the Ford's headlights. Saturday night, but there wasn't much going on in the town: a handful of bars and restaurants open, everything else shut down. Didn't even seem to be much in the way of Christmas lights or decorations.

He found a motel on the southern outskirts, checked in, asked about a place to eat. The woman on the desk recommended a nearby family restaurant that was open till midnight; best food in the county, she said. Runyon doubted it. And the doubt proved out right.

In his room he checked the county phone directory. Bridgeport was twenty miles away. The county courthouse and main library were both open on Mondays, the courthouse at nine A.M. Lee Vining, if

248

he needed to go there, was thirty miles beyond Bridgeport.

He went to bed, tried to sleep, couldn't. Colleen, Joshua, Colleen. He put on the flickery TV, lay there staring at it, waiting for his body to lose its road hum and his mind to finally shut down.

19

Jake Runyon

The address for Robert Lightfoot was a mobile home park built along an aspen-lined stream a few blocks from downtown Bridgeport. Older complex of weathered trailers separated by small, well-kept yards carpeted now with thin layers of snow. Its network of black asphalt streets and courtyards had been swept recently, though there were patches of ice here and there that made driving tricky. The temperature, at a few minutes before ten A.M., was only a couple of degrees above freezing.

Instead of steps, a switchbacked handicap ramp led up to the door of the Lightfoot trailer. Strips of rough, sandpaperlike material made the footing on the ramp more or less secure. The door was set into a glass-fronted porch that offered a partial view of the distant, snow-clogged Sierras. There was a little brass knocker instead of a bell push; Runyon used it twice, didn't get a response either time.

When he came back down the ramp, a woman was standing on the open porch of the trailer across the narrow courtyard. Late sixties, gray-haired, bulbous body encased in a white chenille bathrobe; wool-stockinged legs as thin as pipe stems showed beneath the robe's hem. The overall effect was of a giant shorebird with an inquisitive expression in place of a beak.

Runyon bypassed the Ford, moved slowly across to the edge of her yard. The frigid weather had started a steady ache in his weak leg, but he didn't favor it. He refused to let himself limp, no matter how much the leg hurt. Stubborn pride, Colleen had called it, but she'd understood. There wasn't anything about him she hadn't understood.

"If you're looking for Mr. Lightfoot," the woman said, "he's not home."

"Can you tell me when he'll be back?"

"After services. He's a Methodist."

"Ah."

"They hold services later than we do, the Methodists. I'm Catholic, I've already been to Mass."

"Ah."

"Mrs. Doyle took him about twenty min-

251

utes ago," the woman said. "She cares for him, you know."

"Nurse?"

"Housekeeper. She comes three days a week to clean and cook, and on Sundays she takes him to church."

"He's an invalid, then."

"Confined to a wheelchair, poor man, since his stroke. That was . . . let's see, four years ago. No, five years ago." Her breath plumed. "The older you get, the harder it is to keep track of time."

"Mr. Lightfoot doesn't have any family?"

"Well . . . I don't really know. I suppose not."

Evasive answer. He said, "Lightfoot's not a common name. There's a George Lightfoot in Lee Vining. Maybe they're related."

"They may be. If they are, George Lightfoot doesn't come to visit. In fact," she said pointedly, "Robert hardly has any visitors except for Mrs. Doyle."

"Is that right?"

"He's . . . well, he's not the most neighborly person, poor man. His stroke, you know." She seemed about to add something, changed her mind.

Runyon asked, "How long has he lived here?"

"Since his stroke. He used to live in Aspen Creek, but he had to sell his home. Hospital bills — he didn't have enough insurance. It's criminal, what they charge you for medical care these days. Especially when you're elderly and live on a fixed income, as most of us here in Shady Wood do. Everyone takes advantage of the elderly, or tries to." Another pointed comment. "Salesmen, for instance."

"I'm not a salesman."

"Well, I should hope not. It's the Sabbath, after all."

"Would you know if Mr. Lightfoot had a daughter, or maybe a niece, named Dorothy? Married to a man named Anthony Colton in the early eighties?"

The woman's face went blank, as suddenly as if it had been swept with an eraser. She said, "Why are you asking about that?" in a voice gone as icy as the courtyard asphalt.

"Then he is related to Dorothy Colton?"

"That terrible business again, after all these years. My Lord."

"What terrible business?"

". . . Don't you know?"

"Only that Dorothy Colton died in Aspen Creek in nineteen eighty-five. I'm here to find out how and why, if there's any connection to a man named Vernon Snow who died the same day."

"Why? Who are you?"

"Private investigator," Runyon said. "What happened back then has some bearing on a case my agency is handling in San Francisco."

"What case? What agency?"

He ignored the first question, answered the second. "Any help you can give me . . ."

"You won't get any from me," she said. "I won't talk about it. Not on the Sabbath. And don't you bother Mr. Lightfoot about it, either. Show some mercy, for heaven's sake. That poor man has suffered enough."

She heeled around, disappeared into her trailer. He heard the lock click as soon as the door shut behind her.

On his way out of Shady Wood, Runyon tried his cell phone. It worked, but the signal was weak because of the mountains and the weather; he didn't even try to make a call on it.

Bridgeport, like Aspen Creek, was built along Highway 395. A little larger, dominated by a courthouse at least a century old, many of its other buildings flanking the icebound East Walker River. The downtown streets were festooned with wreaths and candy canes and strings of lights — a town with more life and civic pride, maybe because it was the county seat. He found a café and a public phone, put through a call to George Lightfoot's number in Lee Vining.

A woman answered, told him to wait one moment. He waited a hundred or so before a gruff male voice came on. Runyon identified himself, asked if he was talking to a relative of Robert Lightfoot who used to live in Aspen Creek.

Long silence. Then, warily, "Why you want to know?"

"I'm trying to find out what happened to a woman named Dorothy Lightfoot Colton in August of nineteen eighty-five."

"Christ! Dragging all that up again? Who'd you say you were?"

"A private investigator. Dorothy Colton's name came up in —"

"I don't know nothing about it. He's my asshole cousin, I haven't talked to him in ten years, I don't care if I ever talk to him again. I hardly knew the girl. Can't you just let people forget?"

"Forget what, Mr. Lightfoot? How did she die?"

"Talk to Bob, you want the gory details.

I got nothing to say. Don't call me up again."

Runyon sat in the café drinking tea and letting time pass. At noon he drove back to the mobile home park. Robert Lightfoot was back from church, and apparently alone: the upper body of a man was visible behind the porch glass, and there was no car in the courtyard until Runyon brought the Ford in there. There'd been some blue in the sky earlier; now it was all gray threaded with black, with the cloud ceiling coming down. Colder, too. More snow on the way.

He went up the ramp to the porch door. From there he could see all of the man, in a wheelchair at the far end. A heavy robe was draped loosely across his lap, the chair turned so that he was staring straight back at Runyon. Even at a distance he looked old, shrunken, what hair he had left as white as fresh snow, his face seamed and lined and drawn in on itself like a gourd left too long to dry in the sun. But the eyes were alive, bright and unblinking. Embers glowing hot in whitish ashes.

Runyon tapped on the glass, made a gesture: All right if I come in? The old man's hands were hidden under the robe; he

256

didn't move. Another tap, another gesture. Except for the eyes, Robert Lightfoot might have been dead in the chair.

On impulse Runyon tried the knob. Unlocked. He opened the door, inward to the left; put one foot inside and said, "Mr. Lightfoot, I'm sorry to bother you —"

That was as far as he got, motion and words both. The old man moved more quickly than Runyon would've believed possible. Gnarled hands threw off the robe, came into view clutching a short-barreled pump gun; the slide made an ominous ratchety noise as he jacked a shell into firing position. The muzzle held as steady as if it were clamped in a vise.

"One more step, mister, I'll cut you in two."

Runyon stood stiff and still. The words had come out of the right side of Lightfoot's mouth; the left side seemed to have been frozen by the effects of his stroke. They had a slurred quality, but the threat behind them was stone-hard.

"I mean you no harm. I only want to —"

"Know what you want, you and your goddamn agency." That information had to've come from the bird woman across the way. Leave Lightfoot alone, show some mercy, she'd said, and then shown him

257

none herself. "Won't get it from me."

"If you'll just let me —"

"Only thing I'll let you do is leave. Back out, go away, don't come back. You got five seconds."

Runyon backed out, pulling the door shut as he went. Through the glass the hot eyes and the pump gun's muzzle followed him down the ramp and across to the Ford. He got in without looking back, started the engine, drove away.

Bad scene in there. He'd been under a gun before, but not in a long time — not since the day he and Ron Cain chased the homicide suspect and Ron ended up dead in the car smash. The tension in him was the same, like sparking wires, even though the danger had been fairly small. It would be a while before it eased out of him.

But he'd learned one thing in those few seconds, cemented one connection.

The man who'd called Human Services in San Francisco, the man with the slurred voice, was Robert Lightfoot.

If you wanted information in small towns off the beaten track, taprooms and taverns where the locals hung out were the places to get it. Pick one, nurse a drink, settle on a likely candidate, then play the schmooze game and work the conversation around to where you wanted it to go. He'd developed a knack for it. Or maybe it just came naturally. He'd been the regular type once — good listener, easy rapport with strangers. When he was on the SPD, even after the accident, and pretty much right up until God or whoever pulled the plug on Colleen's life and his along with it.

Back in Bridgeport he spotted a Victorian-style inn on the river, a former stage stop, he found out later, for a place called Bodie that had once been a mining boomtown and was now one of the few remaining authentic ghost towns in the west. The bar lounge was moderately crowded, probably because they had an NFL game on a battery of TVs. He'd been a rabid football fan once, something else he and Colleen had shared. Went to the Dome for Seahawks games whenever they could cadge tickets or afford scalpers' prices, seldom missed one on television. She'd get so excited in the heat of action that her face would turn bright red and she'd start screaming — in the stands or at home, didn't matter where. He still watched games on Sunday, but now it was just something to do to pass the time. All his zest for the game was gone. One more on the list of things lost and gone forever.

Most of the locals were watching the game. He picked a loner like himself, an old-timer down at one end of the bar who didn't seem to be a football fan. Spent the better part of an hour and the price of two drinks schmoozing and pinching out bits and pieces of what had happened in Aspen Creek in 1985. But that was all they were, bits and pieces. Just enough to raise more questions.

At halftime he left and drove through a moderate snowfall back to Aspen Creek, where he should've gone in the first place. Fewer watering holes there, and the first one he tried was a bust. The second, Magruder's Bar and Grill on a street off 395, looked like it would turn out the same until a middle-aged, red-bearded giant in a lumberman's jacket and overalls walked in.

Everybody in there knew the giant, treated him in the raucous way small-towners reserved for local characters. His name was O'Sheel. Friendly, opinionated, profane, with a fondness for pale ale in schooners and the sound of his own voice. All it took for a stranger to prime the pump was to be a good listener and the magic words, "How about another beer?" He wore a lot of local hats: fisherman, wilderness guide, construction worker, handyman. Talked about trout fishing, cross-country skiing, the restoration of Mono Lake, how much he loved the outdoors and hated politicians, taxes, polluters, city-bred environmentalists, the Bureau of Land Management, off-road vehicles, and watered-down beer. And eventually he talked about what Runyon wanted to hear.

"Oh, yeah, sure, I remember that business," he said in his rumbling voice. "Summer of 'eighty-five. You get a lot of whacko shit down in the cities, San Fran, L.A., but not up here. Big goddamn deal up here. People didn't talk about nothing else for weeks, months. Still talk about it, some of us, because it ain't finished yet. All these years, it still ain't finished."

"What happened, exactly?"

"Three people killed, that's what happened. Boom, boom, boom, blew 'em away just like that one afternoon over on Sweetwater Street. Colt forty-one caliber semiauto, now that's some piece, that baby does damage. Blew one of the guys' heads half off, the way I heard it."

"Who did? Who was the shooter?"

"Man named Colton, Tony Colton. Sold insurance for Ed Bateman right here in town. I knew him. Hell, everybody around here did. Nice guy, quiet, never any trouble, you'd've thought he was the last one'd go off his nut and start blowing people away. But you never know. Give a man enough reason, you or me, any man, he's got the potential. It'd been me, my old lady, maybe I'd've done the same thing. Prob'ly not, prob'ly I'd just beat the crap out of her, but who knows? You don't ever know what you might do until you come right up against it, am I right?"

"You're right," Runyon agreed. "So what was Colton's reason?"

"Oldest one there is. Come home when he wasn't supposed to, found his old lady screwing his best friend. Luke Valjean, worked at Sullivan's garage, they were buddies since high school, and there was Luke banging Dottie in the poor bugger's own bed. Dottie Colton, that was her name. Not that you could blame Luke. Pretty woman offers a man a free piece, it ain't easy to turn down. He wasn't the first, neither. That come out later. Usually it's the guy looking to get some strange, am I right? Not this time. Uh-uh. She'd had two, three others before Luke, one a goddamn politician over in Bridgeport. Tony never had a clue, I guess. Must be why he snapped the way he did when he come in and heard that old bed of his singin'."

"Shot them both in bed?"

"Both naked, that's right," O'Sheel said. "Sidearm was Dottie's, belonged to her old man, he taught her how to shoot when she was a little kid. Tony, though, he'd never fired one in his life until that day. Funny, ain't it, him not even liking guns? What's that word they got for something like that?"

"Irony," Runyon said.

"Yeah. Irony. He emptied that Colt, got Dottie once and Luke twice. Blood all over everything. Then he run out the house and that's when the other poor bastard got it."

"Victim number three."

"Right. Neighbor, old Vern Snow. Heard the shots, come running over to see what it was all about. Might be alive today if he'd minded his own business. Got there the same time Tony run out. Tony sees him, Vern gets in the way, and Tony pops him too. Once in the back, shattered his spine. Another D.O.A."

"What'd Colton do then?"

"Jumped in his car and drove off like a bat outta hell. Straight out of town. Straight into the goddamn Twilight Zone."

"The what?"

"That's what somebody said, I forget who."

"You're saying he got away?"

"Clean away. Ask me how that could happen in wide-open country like this, deputies and highway patrolmen everywhere, helicopters, spotter planes, I can't give you an answer. Shouldn't've been possible, but it happened just the same. Found his car abandoned a couple of days later, over in Nevada. But not a trace of Tony, then or since."

"So they never caught him."

"No sir," O'Sheel said. "Straight into the Twilight Zone, like I said. That's why it ain't finished. Seventeen years since Tony Colton blew away his wife and Luke and Vern Snow and they ain't caught him yet, don't have a clue what happened to him. He just plain disappeared."

20

Yet another Tamara showed up for work Monday morning. Last week we'd had Old Tamara, Hurt Tamara, Angry Tamara, Resigned Tamara. Today we had Wistful Tamara. Soft little moans, long gazes into the distance, an expression that seemed to be caught halfway between happiness and melancholy. Men have mood swings. Women have mood leaps, mood swirls, mood loop-de-loops.

"What happened over the weekend?" I asked her.

"I got laid and moved back with Horace."

More information than I wanted. "Well," I said. "So you two had a talk and worked things out."

"No. Uh-uh."

"You didn't? You just said you're back together."

"Living together. Sleeping in the same bed."

"But you still haven't resolved your differences."

"No. Just together for the holidays."

"Then what?"

"Don't know yet."

"You haven't changed your mind about marrying him?"

"No."

"And he hasn't changed his about leaving."

"No. He's going to Philly."

"And you're staying here."

"Probably."

"Probably?"

"What I said."

"Tamara . . ."

"Man loves me, I love him. How can I give him up?"

"You don't have to. Lots of couples have long-distance relationships."

"Not us. Wouldn't work."

I said slowly, "You're not actually considering going with him, are you? Giving up your career here?"

"Got to give up one or the other, sooner or later."

Patience, I told myself, patience. "It'd be a big mistake. Opportunities like the one I offered you don't come along very often."

"I know it."

"It's not me I'm thinking of," I said. "I can go along for a while with Runyon's help, then sell out to him or somebody else when I'm ready for full retirement. What concerns me is you, *your* future."

"Sure. Big Daddy."

It wasn't sarcasm; her tone said she meant the phrase affectionately. "Better give it careful thought before you make a decision. Use your head, not your emotions."

"That's what Claudia says."

"Claudia's right."

"Be the first time, if she is. Don't worry, I'm on it. Not gonna leave you hanging."

"What worries me is you leaving yourself hanging."

The phone ringing put an end to the discussion. Just as well. I might have been able to push the issue with one of the other Tamaras, even Angry Tamara; but Wistful Tamara was off in her own little space, unreachable by a sixty-one-year-old male Caucasian. Even if the sixty-one-year-old male Caucasian were capable of sage advice to the young and lovelorn, which he wasn't. Kerry? She might be. Same sex, same language.

The call was for me. Jack Logan. We spent a minute or so kicking around the retirement thing, then he got down to the real reason for his call.

"Big Dog," he said. "He's no longer a fugitive."

"In custody?"

"In the morgue."

"What happened?"

"Somebody blew him away. Friday night sometime."

"Where?"

"Body was found yesterday morning. Behind a plastics company warehouse on Army, next to a Dumpster. Shot twice with a forty-one caliber weapon."

"Same gun that killed Spook?"

"No report from Ballistics yet — they're backlogged as usual. But you can bet it was the same weapon and the same shooter."

"The wages of blackmail," I said.

"Looks that way. ID on him just came through from NCIC. Joseph Gorley, age forty-six. Ex-navy, thrown out in 'seventynine for drunken misconduct and striking an officer. Long rap sheet dating back to the early 'eighties, mostly D&D and aggravated assault. One less cretin to clutter up the streets and the court system." Harsh assessment, but true enough. Sentimentality in any form is anathema to police work.

"Anything at the scene?"

"Nope. At first it looked like just another street killing, so the tech boys did a cursory. You know how it is with those cases."

"Yeah."

"Once the link was established, we sent a team back out for another sweep. Same result."

"Killed there or somewhere else?"

"There. Bloodstains that the rain didn't wash away, drag marks twenty feet or so to the Dumpster. Driven there on the promise of more money, probably, and paid off with a bullet."

"Double homicide makes it a priority case now, right?"

"Right," Logan said. "Your new guy, Runyon, happen to be in?"

"No. Why?"

"He was out looking for Big Dog the other night. Inspector in charge, Gunderson, turned that up."

"If he saw anything or knew anything, you'd have heard from him by now. He's a by-the-book player, Jack. We wouldn't've hired him if there was any chance he wasn't."

"I'll take your word for it. But I'd still like to talk to him."

"When he comes in, I'll have him call

you. Might be tomorrow sometime."

"No problem."

Tamara had been listening to my end of the conversation. When I put the phone down, she said, "So Big Dog got himself put down."

"Yeah. I don't like the way this case is shaping up. My gut feeling says none of us is going to be happy with the outcome, including our client."

"Long as Mr. Taradash pays the rest of his bill. Want me to try calling Runyon on his cell?"

"Not yet. Give him time to make the rounds up in Mono. Meantime, you might ask Felicia to find out if there's anything on Dorothy Lightfoot and the others in the NCIC."

"Already done. E-mailed her while you were on the phone."

"Is that a good idea? I mean, she could lose her job if the brass finds out she's doing favors outside the department."

"We got us a little code worked out, knamean? Anybody sees that e-mail I just sent, they won't have a clue what it's about."

"My partner, the cryptographer."

"Yeah. Your partner."

And another little moan, another long silent gaze into space.

She worried me, she really did. The thought that Wistful Tamara might knock Sensible Tamara on the head and turn into Trash-Her-Future Tamara was depressing in the extreme. Better get Kerry involved in this right away. If anybody could talk turkey to a stubborn, moody, lovesick, borderline head case, it was Kerry. Hell, she'd had plenty of practice with me all these years, hadn't she?

"No," Kerry said.

"What do you mean, no?"

"What part of the word don't you understand? It's not a good idea."

"Why isn't it?"

"It just isn't. What makes you think she'd listen to me?"

"Voice of experience. You're a woman, she's a woman —"

"Yes, and no woman wants another intruding on her personal life with unsolicited advice. If Tamara were to ask me, fine. But she hasn't."

"I'm asking you. Please."

"No."

"If you'd just . . ."

"What did you say?"

"Dammit!"

"What? I can barely hear you."

"Damn car phone cuts out in parking garages sometimes." I shook the receiver, fiddled with the unit. "Better now?"

"A little. Why are you calling from a parking garage?"

"Well, I couldn't do it from the office, could I, with Tamara right there. I made an excuse and came over here to the car."

"Terrific," she said. "Sneaky games at your age."

"What?"

"Never mind. When are you going to break down and buy yourself a cell phone?"

I ignored that. "So you won't talk to her, not even a few words?"

"Not even one word. Be realistic. What could I tell her? She's young and black and I'm old and white."

"You're not old."

"From Tamara's point of view I'm fodder for assisted living."

"You could tell her not to screw up her life."

"It's her life. Her choices."

"Kerry, listen . . ."

"You listen. Leave her alone. Don't try to interfere, don't try to get anybody else to interfere. Especially not now, with

Christmas so close."

"What does Christmas have to do with it?"

"You want to spoil her holidays?"

"No, but —"

"She's level-headed, she knows what's best for her. And it isn't giving up a good career opportunity to be the wife of a Philadelphia symphony cellist."

"Love's blind, kiddo, or hadn't you heard?"

"Oh, Lord, don't give me clichés. Just trust my instincts. Leave the woman alone, let her work this . . ."

"What? This effing phone . . ."

"Effing," Kerry said. "You really must be upset."

"Of course I'm —"

"What?"

"I said —"

"What? You're cutting out again. Listen, I can't talk any . . . have to . . . work . . . that new ad campaign I . . ."

"What?"

"Just remember . . . told you. Don't inter . . ."

"What?"

Too late. She'd already hung up.

When I came back into the office,

Tamara said, "Felicia just called."

"And?"

"One NCIC hit. Anthony Colton."

"And?"

"Fugitive warrants out on him, state and fed both."

"For what crime?"

"Big enchilada. Homicide, multiple."

"The hell. How many victims?"

"Three. Seventeen years ago in Aspen Creek. Mono County Sheriff's Department put out the original warrant, FBI issued theirs not long after."

"In nineteen eighty-five?"

"Yep. Colton's been at large ever since."

"Details? Victims' names?"

"Not yet. Felicia's got a request in for specifics."

And you never knew how fast you'd get a response on that kind of request. The NCIC processes thousands from law enforcement agencies nationwide every day; the simple ones usually come back fast, detailed case files take longer. It all depended on how busy they were, and on the exact nature of Anthony Colton's crimes and how high on the FBI's fugitives' list he rated after seventeen years.

I said, "Any other felonies on Colton's record?"

"Not in California. Might be a spree."

"Might be. Two of the victims have to be his wife and Vernon Snow."

"And number three's Luke, whoever he was."

"Which makes Anthony Colton —"

"Spook. Uh-huh."

It seemed a stretch until you thought about it, put it in the right perspective. Seventeen years on the run. Unbalanced from the first, riddled with guilt over what he'd done, deteriorating physically and mentally under the strain to the point where he attempted suicide by self-mutilation, finally ended up down and out, addled and harmless, gabbling to the ghosts of his victims on the streets of San Francisco. Who'd figure a passively disturbed homeless man for a fugitive multiple murderer? Well, somebody had. It was the only explanation for his murder that made sense. Whoever had fired that bullet into Spook's head, and then put Big Dog down, was connected in some way to the triple homicide in 1985.

21

Jake Runyon

He was waiting on the steps, huddled against wind and blowing snow, when the Mono County courthouse opened at nine A.M. Vital Statistics, first stop. Not much there. No birth certificate for Luke or Lucas Valjean. Nobody named Valjean residing in the county at present, but two others had died in Aspen Creek within a year of Luke: Everett, age 67, in 1986, and Dinah, age 66, in 1987, both of the same address. Luke's parents? Seemed likely. Vernon Snow had lived in Aspen Creek all his life, been widowed at the time of his death, and had fathered two daughters; one of the daughters had been married in Mammoth Lakes, but there was no current directory listing under her husband's name or her maiden name anywhere in Mono County.

The Sheriff's Department had offices in the courthouse, but Runyon didn't want to walk in there cold. Dealing with newspaper people was a chore he avoided whenever possible. That left the local library. It was open when he got there, and the librarian said yes, they had issues of the weekly Mono County *Register* on microfilm dating back as far as 1985. She set him up in a cubicle, brought the file dates he asked for, and left him alone.

ASPEN CREEK MASSACRE
3 DIE IN SHOOTING, KILLER AT LARGE

Front-page scare headlines in the issue dated four days after the homicides. Grainy photograph of a lean, hollow-cheeked, nondescript man identified as Anthony Colton that bore no resemblance to the ravaged, faceless corpse in the San Francisco city morgue. The news story was a mix of lurid details and provincial, "this kind of thing doesn't happen here" outrage. The facts were pretty much as O'Sheel had outlined them the afternoon before. Anthony Colton's car had been found in the Toiyabe National Forest, a wilderness area across the state line a hundred miles or so from Aspen Creek. California and Nevada authorities had cooperated in the manhunt and the FBI had been called in "for assistance" after the car was found. Sure they had. The FBI didn't assist, they assumed control; and state police agencies squabbled over jurisdiction as often as they cooperated. Confusion, ruffled feathers, and wasted time were the usual result. That and blind luck explained Colton being able to elude capture, find his way out of the mountains and into a hole somewhere.

The follow-up articles rehashed events and expressed frustration and public anger at the continued failure of the authorities to find Anthony Colton. The Mono County sheriff and one of his deputies were quoted; another deputy was mentioned by name. Runyon made a note of those three, and a fourth name: Thomas Valjean, Lucas Valjean's older brother, who at that time had lived in the village of Mono City and operated a well-digging and septic service. He was quoted twice, both angry denunciations of law enforcement efforts.

From the library, Runyon drove back to the courthouse and the county sheriff's offices. Two of the three officers named in the news stories, he was told, including the then-sheriff, were no longer with the department. The third, Lawrence Hickox, was now a senior deputy at the Mammoth Lakes substation, fifty miles to the south.

Runyon hunted up a phone — his cell still wasn't working — and put in a call to the Mammoth Lakes station. Hickox was on duty, and when Runyon said he had new information on Anthony Colton, the deputy sounded eager to see him. They made an appointment for one o'clock.

It was after eleven now. Better check in; they'd be wondering what he'd found out, maybe had something to pass on in return. He made the agency number in San Francisco his second call.

It snowed all the way to Mammoth Lakes, flurries now and then, mostly a light dusting; but the highway was slick and pre-holiday traffic made for even slower speeds. A local radio station, the only one he could get on the car radio, said there would be a partial clearing later in the day but another storm was expected tonight, high winds and up to three inches of snow tomorrow. If he came back up 395 right after the talk with Hickox, he ought to have a fairly easy drive as far as Carson City or Reno. And if the storm held off and road conditions were good in the Sierras, he might even be able to make it all the way back to San Francisco without having to lay over.

Spook's identity was pretty much established now; some sort of corroborating evidence was all that was missing, and Hickox should be able to supply that. In the days when he still had Colleen, the manhunter in him might've chafed at quitting an investigation while parts of it were still hot. Now it just didn't matter. Employee doing a job, grunt taking orders — that was all he was and all he cared to be.

When he finally reached Mammoth Lakes he found himself in an upscale mountain resort community already teeming with holiday ski crowds. SUVs, vans, ski-laden cars clogged its neatly plowed streets; by the time he maneuvered through the traffic and located the sheriff's substation, he was better than fifteen minutes late for his appointment.

Lawrence Hickox didn't seem bothered by the delay. He was in his fifties, ruddy-featured, broad head coated in gray fuzz, friendly manner tempered with reserve. They went into his private office to talk. The reserve faded once Runyon mentioned his background and provided a more detailed rundown on the investigation: two professionals on more or less equal footing.

"Anthony Colton, after all these years," Hickox said. "I figured him for dead long ago."

"I would've, too, in your place."

"Pure crazy luck, him squeezing through the dragnet that summer, disappearing without a trace. Seemed like he *had* to be dead. I mean, he was no Richard Kimble. You know, 'The Fugitive.' Colton wasn't half that smart or resourceful."

"What kind of man was he?"

"Average. Model citizen until the day he snapped. Lived quietly, no bad habits, never in trouble of any kind. Didn't hunt or do much hiking or fishing — didn't have any survivalist skills. I'd love to know how he got out of the Toiyabe after he abandoned his car; we never found anybody who might've given him a ride. By all rights a man like Colton, wandering around in that wilderness, ought to've been dead inside a week. That's what I told those TV people that came sucking around."

"TV people?"

"Scouts for one of those fugitive shows that were popular awhile back — 'America's Most Wanted,' 'Unsolved Mysteries,' one of those. They hung around a few days, asked a stream of questions, then

281

went away and we never heard from them again. Maybe my saying Colton must be dead had something to do with it. More likely, they decided the shootings were too cut and dried, or the sex angle too gamy for TV. Two of the victims naked in the sack when they were shot . . . that'd be hard to adapt for a network show, even these days."

Runyon had nothing to say to that, just nodded.

"So," Hickox said. "You're convinced this dead homeless guy in S.F. is Colton?"

"Everything points to it." He went into more detail: Spook's ghosts, the high school yearbook page, the rest of the trail that had led to Mono County. "SFPD didn't get onto the connection because there was no match when they ran his prints through NCIC."

"That's because he was never officially fingerprinted — no military service, no police record, no sensitive job, etcetera. Things were hectic as all hell at the crime scene that first day, people in and out, but we did manage to lift a few clear latents we were reasonably sure were Colton's. A few others from his office, too. But we had nothing to match them against for verification. Sheriff turned the lot over to the FBI after they came in, but I guess the prints never made it into their database."

"I saw the body in the morgue," Runyon said. "Did Colton have a strawberry birthmark on the upper right arm? A scar a couple of inches long under his chin? Three mutilation scars in the genital area?"

"Birthmark rings a bell." Hickox opened a folder, shuffled through a sheaf of computer printouts. "I pulled up the file after you called. We don't usually put old cases into the system, even unsolved ones, but I made sure the Colton casefile got saved . . . Here we go. Birthmark, upper right arm. Doesn't say if it was strawberry or not, and I don't recall where the information came from. One of the victims' relatives, probably."

"Location seems conclusive enough."

"Agreed." Hickox was still studying one of the printouts. "Nothing here about any scars. Did you say mutilation scars in the genital area?"

"Possibly self-inflicted."

"Suicide attempt? Well, that'd be in character for a man ended up as crazy as you say he was. Bad cuts?"

"Bad enough."

Hickox shook his head. "That kind down there don't heal by themselves. He must've had professional treatment. And if it was a suicide attempt he'd've been held for observation. All that attention . . . and nobody realized he was a wanted man."

"It happens," Runyon said. "People slip through the cracks, homeless and mentally ill more easily than anybody else."

"Sure, but he kept slipping through for seventeen years, Christ knows how many times. Phenomenal run of luck."

"Everybody's luck runs out sooner or later."

"Yeah. Shot with a forty-one caliber weapon, you said?"

"One bullet, back of the head execution-style."

"You think whoever did it knew his real identity?"

"We're not being paid to find out who or why, just the ID."

"I'm asking your personal opinion."

"Then yes, that's what I think. Shooter knew him, had reason to want Anthony Colton dead, not a homeless crazy known as Spook."

"Seventeen years is a long time to nurse that kind of hate."

"Not if you were related to one of his victims."

"That occurred to me, too. Anybody

specific in mind?"

"Robert Lightfoot, for one."

"The wife's father? I didn't know he was still alive."

"Lives in a trailer park in Bridgeport. Had a stroke sometime back, confined to a wheelchair."

"If he's in a wheelchair, that lets him out."

"Not necessarily. He knew Spook was Colton before the shooting. How, I don't know." Runyon explained about the phone call to Human Services. "Lightfoot's involved in the first homicide, if not the second. He threw down on me with a pump gun when I tried to talk to him yesterday."

"Then you make it a two-man operation?"

"Adds up that way. The shooter somebody with just as much motive to want Colton dead."

"Another relative?" Hickox said. "Well . . . maybe. I can think of one who fits the bill."

"Thomas Valjean?"

Raised eyebrow. "You do dig deep, don't you? That's right, Lucas Valjean's brother. According to him, Colton didn't just murder one member of his family that day, he murdered three. Father and mother both died within a year or so of the shootings, couldn't seem to reconcile the loss of their son and just gave up on living. Tom was always a hothead. For a long time afterward he came around the department every few weeks, demanding to know why Colton still hadn't been caught. Once he pitched a scene and we had to put him in a cell to cool off."

"Sounds like a man capable of violence."

"Oh, yeah. Beat up a drunk in a bar fight one time, put him in the hospital. Arrested another time for poaching deer out of season. Big hunter. Collected guns, too, come to think of it."

"You remember if he has a large facial mole? Next to his nose, left side."

"Mole? That's right, sure, Tom has one."

"A man answering that description was in the city a few days before the shooting, hunting for Spook."

"Then Valjean sure does figure to be the shooter, doesn't he."

"I checked the local directory — he doesn't live up here anymore. Any idea where he's living now?"

"Seems to me I heard he got married and moved away," Hickox said. "Offhand I don't recall where, but I know somebody who can probably tell me. Friend he used to go hunting with, lives here in Mammoth Lakes."

Runyon watched the deputy make a call, listened to his side of a three-minute conversation. When the call ended, Hickox said, "They're still in touch. Valjean lives down your way, all right. Vallejo. And he's had a load of hard luck lately — IRS troubles, lost his business, wife left him. Enough right there to shove a man like him to the edge."

"And Colton turning up pushed him over."

"Yeah. Who's handling the homicide investigation at SFPD?"

"Lieutenant Jack Logan's the man to talk to. Friend of one of my bosses. He knows by now that the John Doe was Colton."

"I'll give him a ring, fill him in about the birthmark and the rest of what we've discussed. You want to talk to him?"

"No need. My job's finished — we're out of it now."

"Good job, too. Heading home then, get back in time for Christmas?"

Home. Christmas. Just words.

"Yes," Runyon said. "Heading back to San Francisco."

22

Tamara

Monday night:

Pop said, "Sweetness, why didn't you let us know you and Horace are back together?"

"We're not back together. I was gonna call you —"

"You're sharing the apartment again. What's that if not back together?"

"Temporary arrangement. For the holidays."

"Claudia said —"

"You believe everything she says? Big sister knows all, tells all, can't do no wrong?"

"Now where's this anger coming from? You think we favor Claudia?"

"Well, don't you?"

"Of course not. If that's why you resent her —"

"Only times I resent her is when she

tries to run my life."

"She helped you make peace with Horace, didn't she?"

"What I mean, Pop, what I mean! All she did was make things harder on me."

"I don't understand that."

"Looking to make my decisions, thinks she knows what's best for me. Ever since we were kids."

"And you're saying she's never been right?"

"Sure she has, but that's not the point."

"What is the point? You haven't always made the right decisions on your own, you know."

"You gonna start in on all the crap I put you and Ma through when I was a teenager? My rebellious years?"

"No. Ancient history."

"Uh-huh. Claudia doesn't think so. Still harps on it sometimes."

"Well, she's not perfect either. Nobody is."

"Close to it, though, huh? No rebel in that child."

"Didn't think there was any left in you. Was I wrong?"

"I'm my own woman, Pop. That's what I'm trying to get across."

"I know it. Don't you think we want you

to be independent?"

"Sure, when you approve of what I'm being independent about."

One of the famous Corbin sighs. "Let's not go any more rounds tonight, Tamara. I'm tired, you're tired, we'll just end up saying things we'll both regret. It's almost Christmas, let's have some peace in the family. You are coming down on Christmas Eve?"

"Tradition. You know I wouldn't miss it."

"That's what I like to hear. Horace, too?"

"Both of us. We already talked about it."

"Okay, good. Just tell me how you want us to handle the situation."

"What situation?"

"You and Horace. As a couple? Friends? What?"

"Well, we're still sleeping in the same bed for now."

"For now. What about next month?"

"He's leaving for Philly on the fourth."

"Doesn't answer my question."

"I can't answer it. Not yet."

". . . All right. Promise me one thing?"

"What's that?"

"Good behavior on Christmas Eve. No arguments, no hassles."

"Me spoil the party? Hey, Pop, don't worry. I'll be your sweetness, a perfect little lady. Just like Claudia."

Monday night.

Claudia said, "Well, what was I supposed to tell Pop? You did move back in with Horace. That's getting back together in my book."

"Not mine. Just means we're fucking again."

"For God's sake. I hope you didn't use that language with Pop."

"He knows what the word means."

"Why do you have to be so vulgar?"

"Why do you have to be so tight-assed?"

"You're twenty-five, an adult — act like it."

"Yes, Ma. Okay, Ma."

"Sometimes . . . I think you actually hate me."

"Wrong. No hate for anybody in this girl."

"Resent me, then."

"That's what Pop thinks. Told him only when you try to boss my life."

"I've never tried to boss your life."

"And when you pretend you don't and never did."

A Claudia sigh. Little softer, little more drawn out than one of Pop's. Two of them ought to do a duet, get Horace to play accompaniment on his cello. "Sonata of Sighs in D Flat," something like that.

"Tammie, you know I care about you —"

"Don't call me Tammie. I hate that fool name, knamean?"

"Knamean. That's another thing. Street slang, ebonics . . . half the time you talk like somebody from the projects."

"That what you think I am? Ghetto stereotype?"

"I know you're not. I just wish —"

"What, sistah? That I'd talk white folks' talk like you?"

"I don't 'talk white folks' talk,' I speak correct English. There's a big difference."

"Is there? Yeah, well, it's whitey's world and you just trying to get along."

"That's right," Claudia said, "it is still whitey's world. But it's changing, and I'm trying to do what I can to help. By working within the system."

Lawyer talk now. "And I'm not, that what you're saying?"

"No, that's not what I'm saying. I respect you, the way you've turned your life around. I just want you to fit in —"

"Turned my life around. Fit in. Whoa, girl. Way over rap. Off da hook!"

Sigh. "Are you going to act like this on

Christmas Eve? Spoil the holidays for the rest of us?"

"Just like Pop. Same worry out your mouth."

"What answer did you give him?"

"Gonna be a perfect little lady, just like you."

"I hope you mean that. Are you bringing Horace?"

"Are you bringing the oreo?"

"Brian is *not* an oreo! Stop calling him that. He's a good man, a brilliant attorney, and you'd better get used to him. You're going to be seeing the two of us together for a long time."

"Don't tell me that silky dude proposed to you?"

"Not yet, but he will. Soon."

"Thinking on a big wedding, huh? The whole nine yards?"

"I'd like a formal wedding, yes."

"Whoo. You in a white dress, Brian in a tux — be just like watching a glass of milk and a big old cookie exchanging vows."

". . . God, Tamara, you can be a bitch sometimes!"

"Guess who I learned it from, big sister."

Monday night.

Horace said, "Why do you act like that

with your family?"

"What, you eavesdropping on me now?"

"You were talking loud enough for the neighbors to hear."

"Don't you be ragging on me too."

"I'm not. I'd just like to know why you can't get along with your family, why every conversation has to turn into a sniping match."

"Always my bad, right?"

"I didn't say that."

"Didn't have to. Better stay on your own side the bed tonight."

"So now it's my turn to get chopped."

"Tomorrow night, too."

"Dammit, woman. Did you mean what you said to Claudia and your father?"

"Mean what?"

"We're not really back together, all we're doing is sharing a bed for the time being."

"Well, duh. One day at a time, like you said."

"I know what I said, but I keep hoping . . ."

"That I'll change my mind? Marry you, move back east?"

"Marry me at least. Would that be so bad?"

"Wouldn't be so good."

"What about the promise you made me?"

"What promise?"

"At Claudia's. That you won't give up on us."

"If I'd given up, I wouldn't be here right now."

"But you won't make any kind of commitment."

"Like the one you went and made all by yourself?"

"Baby, it wasn't a choice between you and my music —"

"No? You gonna leave your cello behind when you go?"

"What? Of course not."

"Same way I feel about my job."

"It doesn't have to be us or our careers, one or the other, all or nothing. Why can't you believe that?"

" 'Cause I stopped believing in fairy tales when I was six years old."

Tuesday morning.

Sad and lowdown when she got to the office. Still on edge, too, so it was a good thing the boss man was planning to be out most of the day, business interview and Emily's school pageant, and Jake Runyon wasn't back from Mono yet. She might've gone off on one of them for no good reason, the way she kept doing lately, make herself feel even worse.

Quiet in there, sitting at her desk. Gave her time to scrape around inside her head, take an objective look at what she found. Didn't like it much, but there it was and might as well admit it. Person she was really upset with, person who'd needed bitch-slapping all along, was herself.

Pop, Ma, Claudia, Horace, Bill . . . they all cared about her, wanted good for her. So why did she keep fighting and ragging on them, keep turning into the angry smartmouth like some black-sister Jekyll and Hyde? Oh, they were always so sure they knew what was best, wouldn't let her be her own woman, live her own life her own way. Only problem was, sometimes she ran a little scared. Felt insecure, vulnerable. Didn't know what she should do, didn't feel sure of herself, needed help figuring out what was best for her. Purely hated being dependent on anybody, but those times she just had to reach out. That was why she'd moved in with Claudia when she left Horace, why she'd let him take her to bed last Friday night, why she'd moved back in with him so quick and easy. Why she drove down to Redwood City every few weeks to spend time with the folks. What she partly was, like it or not, was a woman who didn't want to be alone, needed somebody close to lean on. Only she couldn't just lean, uh-uh, not her. The more dependent she became, the more she started hating herself, and blaming other people for her insecurity, and before she knew it she'd lapsed right back into her old 'tude.

No big insight here, she thought ruefully. She'd let herself see clearly before, made vows before to own up and change her ways. But just when she'd make a start in the right direction, something would happen and she'd handle it wrong, words coming out her mouth without going through her brain first, closing off and lashing out at the same time. Like the other day when Pop came to the office, Friday night at Claudia's, the three conversations last night.

Better stop treating everybody like an enemy, girl. Hang on to family, friends, learn self-control, or else you're really gonna end up independent one of these days — gonna end up all alone.

The little slap-talk with herself made her feel better. When Jake Runyon called a few minutes later, to let her know he was on the road and expected to be in the office around one o'clock, she made an effort to be nice to him. Told him again what a good job he'd done up in Mono County. The stroking didn't have much effect; all he said was "Thanks" and "See you later."

She did some work, managed to lose herself in it. But then, around ten, the phone rang a second time. And her mood went sour again.

Breathing. Heavy breathing.

Oh, yeah, that was all she needed now. A perv.

Still breathing. She didn't wait for any more, didn't say anything, just slammed the receiver down.

Phone rang again a few seconds later. She ground her teeth, made herself answer it cool and businesslike.

Same jerkoff chump, breathing like a pig at a trough. But then a raspy voice said, "Don't hang up."

"Well, don't be panting in my ear. Something I can do for you?"

She expected an obscene answer and got ready to slam down even harder, bust his eardrum. But he surprised her. He said angrily, spewing the words, "What's the idea siccing the cops on me?"

"Huh?"

"Can't leave a man alone, always after him, never a minute's peace. Everybody, my wife, the IRS, cops, you people, the bastards you're working for. Who arc they? Who hired you?"

Man! "I don't know what you're talking about."

"You know, all right. Don't give me that crap, I'm not taking any more bullshit from anybody."

"Who is this?"

"You know who I am. Sicced the cops on me. All those years, nobody did anything about it, everything went to hell, whose fault is that? Not mine. Goddamn you people, not mine!"

"Robert Lightfoot? Thomas Valjean?"

"Smart bitch, don't play games with me!"

That made her lose it. She said, "Drop dead, asshole," and hammered the receiver into its cradle, damn near broke it. Next thing she did was open her purse, find the high-frequency whistle Pop had given her years ago. Chump called a third time, she'd huff and puff and really bust his eardrum for him.

But he didn't call again. The phone stayed quiet.

Well, all right. Must've been Valjean;

Lightfoot talked with a slur because of his stroke. Why hadn't the cops arrested Valjean by now? Insufficient evidence, probably. Report the call? Not much point. He hadn't said his name; she was just guessing and the police couldn't act on guesswork. Boss man had drummed that into her head enough times, hadn't he? But if he called again . . .

Meanwhile, back to work. She started preliminary work on a skip-trace for Abe Melikian, a hard-luck bondsman who called the agency whenever one of his low-life clients jumped bail, which seemed often enough to put most bondsmen out of business or at least make them think twice about who they posted bond for. Routine stuff. Interesting when she was in the right mood, boring when she wasn't. Boring today.

An hour's worth of the routine was all she could stand. The only good thing about the hour was that the phone stayed silent. For no damn good reason, she surfed Philadelphia on the Net. Fifth largest city in the country, population 5.8 million . . . too many people in one place. City of Brotherly Love. Yeah, right. Well, they did have an African-American heritage museum, and Philly's Quakers had been active in the abolitionist movement and the underground railroad, so the brotherly love thing had some history anyway. Liberty Bell and Freedom Hall. University of Pennsylvania. Home of the Eagles, Phillies, 76ers. And the Philly Cheesesteak sandwich, just what she needed to help keep her weight under control. Average winter temperature of 33 degrees . . . terrific.

Lots of stuff on the plus side, she supposed, but too many minuses if you were a West Coast woman, a San Francisco woman, a snow-and-freezing-cold-sucks woman. Yeah, and a 49er fan like Pop and Bill and everybody else she knew on this side of the Bay. Root for the Eagles? No way.

Horace could adapt to life back there, sure. Horace didn't care about football or the weather or anything much except classical music. (And me, she thought, don't forget me.) But this child? Shrivel right up and die in a snowbank the first winter.

She sighed. And then grimaced because the sigh sounded just like one of Pop's. Wall clock said it was almost noon. She shut down her Mac, put on her coat, locked up, and went out to lunch.

Tommy's Joint on Van Ness, treated herself to their buffalo burger. Some treat. Tommy's specialty had always been one of her favorites, but she just wasn't hungry today, couldn't even eat half of it. Raining again when she came out, and she'd forgotten to bring her umbrella. Figured. She was dripping by the time she got back to the office.

Inside she hung up her coat, squeezed out her scarf and hung that up too. On her way to her desk, she heard the door open behind her. She thought it was Jake Runyon, took another couple of steps without turning. Next second she heard hard, quick footfalls coming up behind her, metallic objects rattling and clanking together, and that was when she started to turn —

Something cracked against the side of her head, something solid that brought a sunburst of pain and confusion and sent her sprawling headlong across the floor.

23

Steve Taradash was still doing that nervous, quit-smoking trick of his with a package of cigarettes. While I talked I watched him take one from the pack, roll it between thumb and forefinger, lay it on the desk blotter, and go through the slice-and-dice routine with his penknife. In the other chair Meg Lawton kept her eyes on me the whole time, a look of near anguish on her round face.

Eventually I stopped talking. Taradash said, "Rotten cancer sticks," and swept the dismembered weed into his wastebasket. Without any sign of glee this time; his expression was bleak. Mrs. Lawton rubbed her palms over the silky material of her skirt, making a dry rustling sound.

She said, "It's so hard to believe Spook murdered three people in cold blood. My Lord, he seemed so . . . harmless."

"He was by the time you met him. Unstable personality unhinged by one psychotic episode, seventeen years of guilt and remorse and self-hatred."

"Until there wasn't anything left," Taradash said glumly, "but a walking vegetable."

"Horrible," she said. "I almost wish . . ."

"That we'd never found out the truth about him? So do I. Try to make a gesture in the spirit of the holidays, this is what you get. I should've left well enough alone."

"Look at it this way," I said. "If you had, Spook might never have been identified and nobody would've known what became of Anthony Colton. At least now the Mono sheriff's department and the FBI can close their files on the case."

"I suppose you're right. Still . . . oh, hell, don't misunderstand me, you and your people did a good job, I don't begrudge the expense. It's just that I'm feeling disillusioned right now."

"I don't blame you."

"And I can't help wondering if Spook got what he deserved out there in the alley, if Lightfoot and Valjean, if they're the ones responsible, were justified in knocking him off."

"Murder's never justified, Mr. Taradash."

"I'm not so sure I wouldn't've done the

same thing if a member of my family was shot down and I had a crack at the man who pulled the trigger."

"Nobody knows what he'd do in a situation like that until he's confronted with it. All I can say is that most of us wouldn't give in to the impulse."

"I wouldn't," Meg Lawton said. "I could never take a human life, not for *any* reason."

"There's another thing to consider, too. The man who murdered Spook also murdered Big Dog. Double homicide isn't any less heinous than triple homicide . . . he's no better than Anthony Colton. Worse in the eyes of the law because his crimes were premeditated."

"Big Dog," Taradash said. "You think he'd still be dead if I hadn't hired you?"

"No question. He signed his own death warrant before we got involved."

Taradash shook out another cigarette, began the ritual once more. "How'd he know who to blackmail? How'd Spook get recognized in the first place, after seventeen years?"

"No answers to those questions yet. We'll get the rest of the story when the police make an arrest."

"*If* they make an arrest."

"They will. I don't think it'll be long."

Meg Lawton had been staring past her boss, through the window at activity on the warehouse floor — employees readying equipment for another indy film being shot in the city, I'd been told. Abruptly she said, as if a thought had just struck her, "Steve, what about . . . you know, a burial plot for Spook, some kind of marker?"

"You don't expect me to go through with that now?"

"It's not that I expect it . . ."

"We found out who he was, isn't that enough?"

"I don't know. If you think so."

"Well, I don't know either." Taradash jabbed his penknife into the cigarette; tobacco spurted like flecks of dry brown blood. He asked me, "What do you think? Should I go ahead, arrange to bury the poor bastard?"

"Not my call. I didn't know Spook."

"No opinion either way?"

"Sorry, no."

"And where would we put him? Here? Mono County?"

I didn't say anything.

"He was so sad," Meg Lawton said, "so . . . damaged. It's horrible, what he did, but he wasn't really free all those years, was he? Didn't really escape punishment? It just seems to me he ought to have a final resting place."

"Maybe," Taradash said, "maybe you're right, I wish I could make up my mind." He jabbed the knife blade again into the corpse of the cigarette. "I wish it wasn't the Christmas season," he said.

Meg Lawton said, "I'm glad it is."

So was I. For a lot of reasons.

24

Jake Runyon

The one thing he'd never liked about investigative work was surprises. When you knew what was going down, or at least had some advance warning, you could make preparations, plan for contingencies. But when you walked cold into an unexpected situation, it was like being hamstrung — you couldn't act quickly, you needed time to regroup and by then it might be too late. More than anything else he hated being helpless.

This surprise was a bad one, the worst kind. Tamara Corbin sitting slumped at her desk, one hand cradling her head, smears and streaks of blood all down the left side of her face and neck and across the front of her blouse. Hot-eyed stranger standing spraddle-legged in the middle of the office — big, rangy, early forties; beard-stubbled, brown hair jutting wild from a blotchy scalp, big mole on the left side of his nose; wearing a flak jacket and camouflage fatigues and high-lace boots. Paper files and desktop items strewn all over the floor.

And guns everywhere — on the surface of Bill's desk, on the floor, spilling out of an open duffel bag next to the desk. At least three handguns, an assembled assault rifle, a couple of big, rapid-fire machine pistols. The piece held steady in the man's hand was a Micro Uzi SMG, which meant a magazine capacity of twenty rounds minimum of 9 mm parabellum ammo. Bad enough if it was semiautomatic, worse if it was automatic. Deadly as hell in any case. There was ammunition spread around, too, boxes of it for all the weapons.

Runyon took it all in, the details and implications, in the few frozen seconds after his entry. Hostage situation, suicide mission, planned slaughter. It shut him down inside, put him on cold alert. Emotion, any kind, was a liability in this type of situation. The only possible survival mechanisms were intelligence, training, instinct. And they were damned puny against a heavily armed man with death on his mind.

The stranger broke the tableau with a sharp motion of the Uzi and raspy words that seemed to come from deeper within him than his diaphragm. "Which one're you? What's your name?"

"Runyon."

"Yeah. Shut the door, Runyon. Lock it again."

He did that, turned around. "Who're you?"

"Three guesses, first two don't count. Who am I?"

"Tom Valjean."

"Right the first time, you people are so fucking smart." Valjean used his free hand to drag the chair away from Bill's desk, then gave it a kick that sent it rattling across the floor. It banged into a corner of Tamara's desk, caromed off; the noise made her jerk, raise her head in an unfocused stare. "Go on over there, smart guy, sit down and keep your hands where I can see them."

Runyon obeyed, moving slow. He asked Tamara, "You okay?"

"Head hurts. Still kind of woozy." Her eyes were on him now, trying to hold him in focus. He saw pain, fear, disorientation — and anger. The anger was good, as long as she kept it under control. Tough kid. If she hadn't come unglued by now, she probably wouldn't. "Cut my face when he smacked me. Won't stop bleeding."

"Doesn't look too bad. Just keep putting pressure on it."

"Shut up," Valjean said. "Don't talk to her, you want to talk you talk to me, understand?"

"Why the arsenal, Tom?"

"Don't call me Tom, all you bastards think you know me, you don't know anything about me."

"What're you planning to do?"

A sly look reshaped Valjean's long, slab-cheeked face. "You're a hotshot detective, you figured out about Colton, all about me and Bob Lightfoot, ought to be easy to figure out about this. Go on, smart guy, figure it out, tell me what I'm gonna do."

Spook had murdered three people in cold blood, lived for seventeen years with their ghosts in his head, but Thomas Valjean was more unbalanced and far more lethal — the real spook in this business. Runyon said, "Colton deserved to die," making the lie sound as convincing as he could. "If he'd destroyed my family, I'd've killed him too. Same goes for Big Dog."

"Drunken blackmailing bastard. Bob and me, we shouldn't've paid him the first time, should've known he'd be back for more. Should've just blown him right out of the picture then."

"Sure. You were justified with both of them."

"Damn right I was."

"But not this time."

"This time, too. Damn right. Dogging me, siccing the cops on me, you're no better than Colton or Big Dog or the rest."

"Cops would've figured out about you and Lightfoot, even if we hadn't."

"Hell they would. Stupid bastards. *You* people, you're the smart ones, Bob told me it was you. You deserve what you're gonna get, same as the others."

"All right. But why not just kill me? I tracked you down, I put the law on you, I'm the one you want. Let the woman go."

"No. She's part of it, you're all part of it."

"Let her go, Tom."

"Nobody leaves, everybody pays." Valjean began to pace the width of the office in short, agitated strides, like an ungainly animal. For part of each crossing, the Uzi was pointing away from where Runyon sat; but there was too much distance between them to try to rush him. He and Tamara would both be dead before he got halfway.

"Bastards who hired you," Valjean said,

pacing, "they're gonna pay too. Who are they, who sent you after me?"

Tamara said, "I wouldn't tell him."

"Runyon hadn't come in when he did, you'd've told me all right. I'd've knocked it out of you."

"He tore up the office trying to find out," she said to Runyon.

"Shut up. You tell me, smart guy. Right now, or I'll bust the other side of her head, make her bleed some more. You want that?"

"No."

"Then tell me who hired you!"

"The Department of Human Services."

"Who? What the hell's that?"

"City agency that administers to the homeless. They didn't know who Spook was and the police weren't getting anywhere, so they brought us in."

"Bullshit. Why would the city care?"

"So he could have a proper burial."

"You're lying to me. Those people, bureaucrats, government bastards, they don't care about homeless people, they don't give a shit about anybody. They're like the IRS, like Marjorie, take your business away, take everything that's left and leave you with nothing, ruin your life."

"You asked me who hired us, I told you.

313

The Department of Human Services."

"*Who* in the department? Who called up, who'd you talk to, give me some names."

"I can't do that."

"You damn well better. Give me a name, then you call them up, tell them get their asses over here."

"Bring in more innocent people so you can murder them? I won't do that, Tom."

"I won't either," Tamara said. "Believe it, man."

Valjean stopped pacing, leveled the Uzi again. "I'll kill you, you don't do what I tell you!"

"You're planning to kill us anyway. But nobody else is going to die if we can help it."

"You can't help it. Cops'll come when you're all dead, SWAT team, you think I care? I'll take some of them out too, as many as I can before they get me."

"Why?"

"Why? I've had it, that's why, I can't stand it any more. All the lies, laws, bullshit, everything, everybody, you hear me?"

"Take out as many people as you can just because you're pissed off at the world. Innocent people doing their jobs."

"Don't tell me that! Innocent! Just doing

your jobs, just following orders, that's what you all say, all you bastards, come around and take away everything a man has, ruin his life, then tell him it's nothing personal, you're just doing your jobs. Well I'm making it personal. I made it personal with Colton and that blackmailing son of a bitch Big Dog and Marjorie and I'll make it personal with you and the bastards that hired you, everybody gets in my way, no mercy no prisoners no more bullshit!"

Tamara made a small noise in her throat. Runyon didn't look at her. Valjean's eyes were smoky at the edges, the pupils as red-black as burning embers; and they didn't blink, he hadn't blinked more than once the entire time. Bad sign. So was the way he kept caressing the Uzi with his free hand, slow, sensuous movements, the intimate caresses of a man making love to a woman. Ready to blow any second, like a shaken bottle of nitro. Anything might set him off — a word, an action, one of his own shorted circuits.

The accelerated rasp of Valjean's breathing and the steady patter of rain on the skylights were the only sounds in there now. Runyon sat tense and spring-coiled. If Valjean blew, there wouldn't be time to do much of anything, but at least he'd be up and trying to get in front of Tamara Corbin. He damn well didn't want to die sitting passive in a chair.

Fifteen seconds like that, and then the crisis point passed. Runyon felt it, saw it in the hot eyes, heard it in the sudden gusty expulsion of breath. Valjean took his left hand off the gun, sleeved sweat from his forehead.

"All right," he said, "all right, when's the other one coming?"

"What other one?"

"Don't play dumb, Runyon, I told you I won't put up with any more bullshit. Three of you work here, when's the other one coming?"

"I don't know. Maybe he won't be in today."

"He's coming, she said he was."

"Later," Tamara said. "Not until later."

"Later, later, *when* later?"

"Told you, man, I don't know."

"Call him, get him on the phone."

"Don't know where he is. Told you that too."

"You must know, you work for him."

"We're partners."

"What? You? Partners?"

"Yeah, me. Young black bitch, how about that?"

316

"Shut up, I didn't mean it that way. You think I'm prejudiced? I'm not."

"You just hate everybody, right?"

"That's right, everybody's equal in my eyes, I hate everybody regardless of race, creed, or color." Valjean laughed, a sound like heavy wheels rumbling through gravel. "Justified, by God. Justified!"

Runyon said, "What happens now?"

"What do you think? We wait for your partner."

"He's not my partner. I just work here."

"You think I care? I don't care about anything any more. It's almost finished. Soon as he gets here, then everybody gets what's coming to them, everybody pays, everybody dies."

25

From Visuals, Inc. I drove downtown and hung around Bates and Carpenter's offices on lower Geary until Kerry could break free. We had just enough time for a quick lunch before we headed out to the avenues to Emily's school. The Christmas pageant was scheduled for one o'clock. She really wanted us to be there, and I'd rather have cut off an arm than add another disappointment to her already too-long list.

The auditorium was mostly full by the time we walked in, but it turned out that the Simpsons, Carla's parents, had saved a couple of seats for us. Nice people, Carl and Lorraine; always cheerful and friendly, and affectionate toward each other in public. But since Emily had dropped her little bombshell, I'd felt uncomfortable in their presence. The Simpsons' problems in the bedroom were none of my business, but the seed had been planted and it kept sprouting whenever I saw them. Out of the mouths of babes. The less you know about somebody else's sex life, the better off you are — and if that isn't an axiom, it ought to be.

So I sat next to Carl and made polite conversation and was relieved when the program finally started. I'd figured they would put it on by grades, but they had a better scheme than that — a series of nonsecular skits, each one integrating several kids from different age and ethnic groups. Pretty well done, too. The second was a Santa's Workshop thing, a biggish twelve-year-old dressed up as St. Nick (poor kid), a dozen or more elves in costume puttering and singing. Originally Emily had been assigned to that skit, in the role of one of the elves, but she'd talked her way out of it. "I think it's silly," she'd said when I asked her why.

"What's silly about it?"

"Elves are silly. There aren't any such things."

"There aren't, huh? What about Santa Claus?"

"He's just a figment."

"Figment?"

"Make-believe. I've known that since I was five."

"Who told you?"

"My mom. She said all that stuff, Santa Claus and reindeer and elves, was just a big stupid fantasy that messes up kids' heads. Parents and friends give you presents at Christmas, not some fat elf in a sleigh."

"You really believe it's just a big stupid fantasy?"

"Well, I cried when she told me. But I'm too old for that stuff now anyway."

Ten years of life. Too old for that stuff. Kids grow up so damn fast these days, by necessity, and maybe the earlier they start being fed doses of reality, the more effectively they'll be able to cope with the screwed-up world of the twenty-first century. Some modern theories of child-rearing embrace that approach. Admittedly Kerry and I are Johnny-come-latelys to parenthood, and I'm hopelessly old-fashioned; but it seems to me that the traditional fantasy beliefs of childhood are neither stupid nor harmful. They encourage kids to indulge their imaginations, allow them to keep their sense of innocent wonder a little longer. Emily's parents had been fearful, cold, materialistic people with darkly hidden pasts; their doses of reality had been tainted and had tainted her. It would be foolish to say that she'd have fewer psychological scars if they'd let her believe in Santa Claus, but in my view, destroying her child's fantasy world so early and so harshly had contributed to the damage.

The skit Emily had lobbied for, and gotten to perform in with Carla Simpson, was called Evening Carolers and featured a wintry street scene — cotton batting and white confetti doing duty as snow — and a dozen or so kids in snowsuit costumes going from door to door singing "Silent Night" and "O Come All Ye Faithful" and "It Came Upon a Midnight Clear." It was the right venue for her, the one she should've been picked for in the beginning. She had a clear, sweet voice and she liked to sing — a fact neither Kerry nor I had known until recently, when she began to come out of herself and regain optimism, put trust in her new life. One night we'd heard her singing in her bedroom, to the accompaniment of one of her CDs: wounded little bird learning how to be happy again. It hadn't taken much praise and encouragement for her to overcome her shyness and do some warbling in front of us; and now, up there on the stage in front of several hundred people, she was radiant and you could tell even at a distance that she was having a fine time. Natural-born performer.

After the show, when kids joined parents out front, she hugged Kerry and me and said, "I'm so glad you're here," as if she'd been worried right up to the last minute that one or both of us would back out.

"So are we," I said. "You were pretty terrific up there, kiddo."

"Honest? I missed a couple of high notes. But so did Carla."

"Couldn't tell it from where we were sitting." Kerry gave me a wink that said, How would you know, you have a tin ear. I ignored it. "How about singing those three carols for us on Christmas Eve, see if you can hit the notes you missed?"

"What, the whole group?"

"We don't need the whole group. Just you."

"Well . . . maybe." But her smile said the suggestion delighted her.

The Simpsons came up. "We're heading home to get things ready for the party," Lorraine said. "Emily's coming with us, right?"

"Right," Kerry said.

Carla said, "Great. See you both around five."

When they were gone again, the two

children in tow, I said to Kerry, "Party? What party?"

"You're a nice man and a good father, you know that? And I love you."

"Never mind the soft soap. What party?"

"The Simpsons are having a little Christmas get-together at their place, kids and adults both. And before you start grumbling and grousing, I'm going to be as nice to you as you were to Emily just now. I'll go by myself and tell them how sorry you are to miss it but you had some urgent business to attend to downtown."

"You're really willing to do that?"

"Well, I don't like to lie, but it's better than listening to you grumble about having to endure another party."

I kissed her, by way of thanks. But in the car, on the way downtown, I began to feel a little guilty. I asked how many people were going to be at the Simpsons'; she said she thought twenty or so. Twenty or so, a third of them kids — not so bad, really. What're they having to eat? I asked then. Canapes, cake, ice cream, she said. Eggnog? Eggnog, sure, what would a Christmas party be without eggnog.

It was the eggnog that did it. I like the stuff, entirely too much. Hard to find and therefore easily avoidable most of the year, but the holiday season is a different story. "All right," I said when I pulled to the curb in front of Bates and Carpenter's building. "You won't have to lie for me. I'll bite the bullet and go to the Simpsons'."

"If you want to," she said. "Entirely up to you. I should be there no later than five-thirty." She slid out of the car, then leaned back inside to wink at me again before she hurried away, a big, broad wink this time.

Sneaky woman. She'd planned it this way all along.

I drove over to O'Farrell, found parking on the street for a change, went into my building. The office door was locked; Tamara must've gone out somewhere. I was smiling, thinking about Emily and her pageant performance, Kerry and her devious little ways, anticipating the Simpsons' eggnog if not the Simpsons' party, as I keyed the door open and walked in.

My high spirits made the shock even greater. It was like passing through a doorway from heaven into hell.

26

Nobody moved, nobody said anything.

It took me a few seconds to absorb the scene, assess it, come to terms with it. The blood on Tamara, the display of weaponry, the look on the stranger's face built a virulent mixture of sickness and profound outrage. I made an effort to keep it from showing, to maintain a neutral expression to match the one Jake Runyon wore over in my desk chair.

The telephone rang.

In the frozen silence the noise was explosive. We all jumped, stared; the tension in the room seemed palpable, pastelike. Sweat had already begun to run on me, warm and slimy, like the feel of a snail track.

"Don't touch it," the guy with the gun said, "let it ring."

Two, three, four . . .

"No, wait a minute, maybe it's those bastards at Human Services. You, Tamara,

325

pick up over there. That's who it is, you tell them get over here right now, make up some excuse, just get them here."

She hesitated. Most of the blood on her face and blouse appeared to be darkening, coagulating. From a not-too-recent wound on her left temple, under the hairline. In some pain, from her expression, but alert, clear-eyed. And in control.

"I'm all right," she said, as if reading my thoughts.

"Answer the fucking phone!"

She lifted her extension. The only item other than weapons and ammunition left on my desktop was the other phone; the gunman picked up at the same time with his free hand.

Don't let it be Kerry, I thought. Please, God, don't let it be Kerry.

Tamara gave the agency's name, listened, said, "No, Mr. Bauer, he's not here. Not expected back today."

Sam Bauer, head of Coast States Insurance's claims department.

"Soon as he comes in tomorrow, right, I'll tell him." Pause. Then, with a bitter edge just before she disconnected, "Merry Christmas to you too."

The receiver on my phone clattered down, hard enough to bring a single ring

326

from the bell. He said to me, "You, you're Bill?"

"And you're Thomas Valjean."

"Smart guy. Everybody's so goddamn smart in this place. Close that door, lock it again, hurry up."

I closed it, locked it. As I turned, my eye caught Runyon's; our gazes locked. He'd been in deadly force situations before, just as I had, but this had to be something new for him too — unstable, heavily armed man bent on a destructive siege. Valjean radiated hate; you could almost smell it in the office along with the stink of sweat and gun oil. On full alert, all his senses heightened. Everything in his favor, nothing in ours. Death was a heartbeat away. And the three of us had no means of communication except by eye contact and maybe careful gesture, nothing to rely on except instinct and luck and the hunger for survival.

I said to Valjean, "What's this all about?"

"You're such a smart guy, you figure it out."

"My fault," Tamara said. "He called before he showed up, started ragging on me, and I slammed his ear."

"Not your fault," Runyon said. "He was coming anyway."

"That's right. I was coming anyway."

"Why?" I said. "Why us?"

"Why do you think? You sicced the cops on me. You and those Human Services bastards."

Runyon said, "I told him that's who hired us. Department of Human Services."

Valjean jabbed the gun in my direction. "Straight talk or more bullshit?"

"Straight. They're our clients."

"Who do you deal with over there? I want a name."

"It won't do you any good."

"Goddamn it, I'm not going to screw around with you people anymore, I want a name!" Growing agitated, fingertip beginning to slide back and forth along the weapon's trigger, veins bulging in his forehead, cords bulging in his neck, eyes like holes in the wall of a furnace. "Give me a name, *now!*"

"Ray Chandler," I said.

"Chandler, all right, Chandler, call him up, get him over here."

"I can't do that."

"I won't tell you again, call him up!"

"He won't be there. Nobody's at Human Services now."

"What kind of crap is that?"

"It's after three. Their offices are closed."

"I warned you, no more bullshit!"

"It's Christmas week. All city offices close early this week."

Fiery stare, his teeth clenched so tight I could see white ridges of muscle on both sides of his jaw. If he called the bluff, demanded one of us make the call, I'd be the one to do it; he didn't know the number over there, and there were a couple of other offices I could call that would likely be empty this time of day. But if he checked first to make sure it was the right number . . .

He didn't call the bluff. He said, "Lousy government bastards, take everything away from other people, average joes, people just trying to get along, keep all the perks for themselves. Christ, I wish I could fix them all, line 'em up and shoot 'em down one by one."

Thought processes muddied by his hate; reacting with some clarity of focus but not anticipating, not thinking things through logically. And not quite ready yet to begin his killing spree. Thin thread of something — humanity, conscience, sanity — holding him back for the moment. But only for the moment. That thread would snap before long. A word, an action, something would break it, or it would just disintegrate from the strain.

Keep him talking. Talk had bought time already or Tamara and Runyon wouldn't still be alive. There was still a chance he'd make a mistake, as keyed up as he was, or that one of us could figure a way to neutralize the threat. So far I couldn't see any gamble worth taking. If Runyon had, it didn't show on his face.

I said, "What did they do to you, Thomas, that you hate them so much?"

"Don't call me Thomas, I don't like it."

"Tom, then. That okay?"

"No, it's not okay. You want to call me something, you call me Mr. Valjean."

"What did the government do to you, Mr. Valjean?"

"Ruined my life, that's what they did."

"How did they do that?"

"Took everything away from me for back taxes. Lousy economy, bitch wife of mine always throwing money away, bastards wouldn't let me have another extension, kept tacking on penalties, then they slapped a lien on the house, on my business, forced me into bankruptcy. What they didn't get Marjorie got when she walked out on me. But I took care of her, all right, I fixed her wagon."

"How'd you do that?"

"Figure it out, smart guy. What you think I did when I went over to her apartment this morning, before I came here? Huh? You tell me."

Runyon said, "So now you've killed three people. Same as Anthony Colton."

"So what? You think I'm no better than he was?"

"I didn't say that."

"Wasn't justified, what he did. My three are. Three of you will be too. And all the rest after you, three more or thirty more."

Get him off that. He was agitated again, increasing tension on the thread. I threw a non sequitur at him: "How'd you find out about Colton?"

"What?"

"Colton. Spook. How'd you find out he was alive, living on the streets?"

"Why do you care how?"

"I'd like to know myself," Runyon said. "You bump into him one day, recognize him?"

"Smart bastards didn't figure out that part? Not so smart after all." Valjean's finger had quit moving, eased off pressure on the machine pistol's trigger. Thread still holding. "All right, you want to know, I'll tell you, then you can all die happy. No, I never bumped into him, I thought he was dead a long time ago. It was that black-mailing son of a bitch, he's the one found out."

"Big Dog?"

"Yeah, Big Dog. Found some crap belonged to Colton, newspaper stories about what he did to Luke and Dot."

"Spook's stash."

"Colton talked to them like they were still alive, Big Dog heard the names, same names in the newspaper stories. Even a stupid bastard like him could put two and two together."

My desk chair gave a sudden low squeak. Runyon shifting position, lifting his hands to drywash his slick face. It didn't mean anything to Valjean, but it struck me as an uncharacteristic gesture. I positioned my head so I could look at Valjean and watch Runyon at the same time.

I said, "How'd he know to contact you?"

Valjean didn't seem to hear that. He muttered, "Talked to them, for Christ's sake. Blew them away that day, walked in there and emptied that Colt into them. My brother . . . wasn't anything left of his face, one of the slugs took his head half off. Killed them and got away with it, seventeen years, and he was still talking to them like they were alive!"

When Runyon lowered his hands again, he let the left one drop to his lap and the right one rest on the edge of Tamara's desk. The only things within his reach were her computer screen and keyboard, the keyboard on the sliding panel just below desktop level. His gaze slid my way long enough to tell that I was watching, then eased the other way to catch Tamara's. She was looking, too.

I repeated my question to Valjean. "How did Big Dog know to contact you? Something else in Spook's stash?"

"Not me, smart guy. He didn't come to me, not the first time."

"Robert Lightfoot?"

"Yeah, Bob. He used to sell cars, had business cards and Colton kept one, who the hell knows why. Big Dog tracked Bob down, said he knew where Colton was, wanted five hundred bucks to say where. Bob called me. We didn't pay him, not right away. He spilled just enough to Bob, we figured we could find Colton ourselves."

"But you didn't."

"No. We decided it'd be quicker to just pay the five hundred, so I met the bastard and gave him his blood money. Stupid.

Should've punched his ticket for him then and there."

Runyon's hand was moving on the desktop, so slowly you wouldn't notice unless you were paying close attention. When it crawled down a few inches onto the sliding panel, I realized what he was after: the mouse attached to the keyboard. His fingers came to rest next to it, near enough for him to lift his index finger and tap it once. He was looking at Tamara as he did it. I thought I saw her give a slight nod in return.

"You do it alone, shoot Colton?" I said. I moved a cautious half pace to my left as I spoke. Valjean didn't seem to notice that, either.

"Yeah, alone. Bob wanted to be there to see it but he couldn't, he's in a wheelchair, so I did the job myself. Finally gave Colton what he had coming for what he did to Bob and me, Luke and Dottie and my folks, all of us, finally some justice after seventeen years. Payback, by God, eye for an eye. Colton and Big Dog and Marjorie and you three and anybody else gets in my way."

Abruptly he began to pace. Crosswise behind my desk to within a couple of paces of the far side wall, turn, back across to the near side wall, turn. Head tilted sideways, eyes flicking watchfully over the three of us as he moved, his lips forming words that now only he could hear. Working himself up to it, the thread getting closer to the snapping point. I had the clear, chill feeling that when he decided to stop pacing, he would start shooting.

Tamara had maneuvered her hand and arm onto the keyboard, and her fingers were slowly loosening the mouse cord-connector. Runyon's gaze met mine again; when Valjean made a turn away from him he nodded once, as imperceptibly as Tamara had, to let me know he was ready.

I moved another few inches to my left on Valjean's next turn. For most of his back-and-forth path, my desk was between the two of us; but when he went into his pivot at the near wall, there were a dozen feet of open floor space separating us. A dozen feet . . . like a hundred yards of no man's land. I waited until he turned back the other way, looked at Runyon and made a couple of small motions with my head, one at the wall, the other at the floor.

Tamara had the mouse connector free of its socket.

Valjean was still pacing, not as rapidly now, no longer muttering to himself.

Runyon's fingers closed around the mouse.

I widened my stance slightly, slid my left foot back a few inches, and held a breath, thinking *Here we go.*

Valjean was looking halfway between me and the others, so that he could keep all three of us within the range of his vision. If he saw any of the calculated movements we made, they didn't register, didn't put a hitch in his step. Three paces from the near wall, he about-faced again, an almost military heel-and-toe turn.

And in that second —

Runyon swept up and threw the mouse sidearm, all in one motion — not at Valjean but past and behind him, its cord flapping and twisting like the tail of a whip.

Tamara cut loose with a banshee shriek, so loud and shrill it was a pressure in the ear.

Valjean pulled up short, his stubbled face registering confusion, his attention caught by her and Runyon and the flying mouse — no longer seeing me at all.

I charged him, head down, body bent as low to the floor as I could get and still make speed.

He heard me coming halfway, spun in

my direction. The machine pistol was a semiautomatic; it chattered two or three times, but confusion and haste and the weight of the thing and the high angle of its muzzle threw all the slugs past me by a couple of feet. Runyon was coming by then; I didn't see him until he slammed into Valjean, throwing the gunarm up just as the pistol hammered again. I barreled into Valjean from my side, the two of us sandwiching him, and we all went down in a wild tangle of arms and legs and squirming bodies. Behind us something heavy and metallic made a thunderous crashing noise; I could feel the vibration in the floorboards as I clawed a grip on the gun . . . hot metal, burning my fingers. I yanked it loose of Valjean's grasp, threw it behind me.

Runyon had the other arm and the big struggling body pinned. I heaved up and back to get leverage and hit Valjean in the face with as much force as I could muster. It hurt him, brought a grunt of pain and weakened his struggles. I slammed him again, a side-swipe blow to the temple so solid that it popped one of my knuckles — a sharp pain I barely felt. The fight began to go out of him. Runyon's turn: one, two shots to the face, the second on the point of the jaw. Valjean stiffened for an instant, went limp all at once. Down and out.

It was over.

The two of us lay draped over him for a few seconds, sucking wind. Then I lifted up again, onto my knees, and yelled, "Tamara!" Tried to yell it, but it came out in a hoarse croak.

I saw her before she answered. She must've thrown herself down and under her desk after she screamed; now she came crawling out. "Not hurt. You? Jake?"

"Okay," I said.

"Okay," he said.

There was a pair of handcuffs in the bottom catch-all drawer of my desk. I didn't have to tell Tamara to get them; she was already crawling that way. Runyon rolled Valjean over, and I yanked his arms behind him and snapped steel around both wrists a few seconds later.

It took a couple of tries to get up on my feet, a little effort to stay there. I leaned a hand against the desk to steady myself, jerked back because of a flash of pain in my popped knuckle, and switched support to the other hand. Runyon was up, too. Except for a grayish tone to his skin, you couldn't tell that he'd come within inches of dying. Tamara's eyes were huge, a lot of white showing, and there was blood on her lower lip that hadn't been there before — fresh blood where she'd bitten through the skin.

Runyon said to her, "Good job with that scream. Helped with the distraction."

"Yeah, well, wasn't all good. I think I peed in my panty hose."

"Damn lucky, all of us. If we hadn't been on the same page . . ."

"But we were," I said.

There were noises out in the hallway, but nobody tried to come inside. The air was hazy with aftersmoke from the fired rounds and foul with the stink of burnt powder. I saw holes in the plaster next to the door, another in the door itself. Saw something else, then — the source of the booming crash of metal that had shaken the floor. One or more slugs from that last burst had taken down the old, ugly chandelier that had hung between the skylights. It no longer looked like an upside-down grappling hook surrounded by clusters of brass testicles; now it was just a mangled pile of scrap.

Tamara said, "I always hated that thing."

"So did I."

"Place'll never be the same again."

"No. No, it won't."

The three of us stood there, looking at each other.

"Sweet Lord Jesus," she said.

CHRISTMAS

Tamara

She hadn't been looking forward to Christmas Eve, but it turned out all right. Better than all right. Everybody being nice to her because of what'd happened on Tuesday, tiptoeing around, avoiding the subject. Good thing; wasn't anything to say that hadn't already been said ten times. Like Ma going off about criminals and lunatics running loose and how she couldn't sleep as it was, worrying about Pop all the time; Pop saying okay, if his youngest daughter insisted on doing detective work, then she'd better start keeping a handgun and learning how to use it; Claudia rapping about the evils of guns and urging her to join the gun-control group she and Brian belonged to; Horace trying to talk her into going into another line of work, any kind of computer job where her life wouldn't be at risk.

But not tonight. Tonight there was a tree

big as ever, all tinseled and strung with lights, and wine, and too much food — ham, roast beef, salads, cookies, pumpkin pie, sweet potato pie — and talk about music, politics, football, all sorts of neutral stuff. Ma was happy because the family was all together and she was doing her homey thing; Pop was happy because Sweetness wasn't being smartass and disruptive; Horace was happy because of all the food and because his girlfriend wasn't being smartass and disruptive; Claudia was happy because her little sister wasn't being smartass and disruptive and because she was with her oreo (no, be fair now, Brian wasn't so bad once you got him out of a three-piece suit and away from a lawsuit), two of them holding hands and eye-humping each other the whole time. And she was happy because she'd quit letting everything get under her skin, quit fighting herself and the people around her, just started going with the flow.

Ever since Tuesday, she'd felt like a different person. Scared as hell while it was going down, shaken up for a while afterward, and then cool with it. Somehow easy in her mind. Sort of . . . what was the boss man's word? Mellow. Right, sort of mellow. Even if it didn't last, she liked the feeling.

It was like when she was a teenager and she and her girlfriends used to smoke J's, only this was a legal high, a natural high.

Dinner, presents, talk, dessert, more talk: the time slid by fast and easy. Seemed they'd just got there and then they were at the door, exchanging hugs and kisses, saying good-bye. She even let Brian kiss her, half on the mouth. Whoo. She must be about half stoned.

In the car as they started back to the city Horace said, "Really nice this year. Everybody seemed to be having a good time."

"Yup."

"But you didn't say much. Sure you're okay?"

"Yup."

"Well, you seemed . . . I don't know, not subdued exactly . . ."

"Mellow?"

"That's it. Mellow. How much wine did you have?"

"One glass. How about we put on a CD?"

"What would you like to hear?"

"Classical. Yo-Yo Ma."

She picked one at random, slid it in. Beethoven, *Symphony #5 in C Minor, Opus 67*. Recognized it on account of she liked classical music. Didn't say so to friends, family, wouldn't even admit it to Horace half the time; wasn't supposed to be cool to like long-dead white guys' music, or much of any kind except rap and jazz. So all right, so she wasn't cool sometimes. Who cared?

In the flicker and shine of passing head-lights she watched Horace listening to the cello passages, his ugly face almost hand-some. A tenderness came into her. She loved him, no question about that. He was her man. Always would be, one way or an-other. But the thing was, the relationship she had with her job and with Bill was an-other kind of love, almost as deep in its own way. Tuesday afternoon, what they'd shared . . . you couldn't get much closer, more intimate. Jake Runyon had been part of it, too. Three of them working together, a unit, a team . . . kind of a professional *ménage à trois*. That was the only reason they were all alive right now.

So she was staying home, just as she'd pretty much known all along she would. The Bay Area was her center, the place she belonged. But that didn't mean she was giving up on Horace. After he left for Philly, well, maybe they *could* keep up a long-distance relationship, for a while anyway. Wouldn't be easy, but love was never easy. She'd always hated that Bobby McFerrin song, but hey, could be the message had some truth after all. Don't worry, be happy.

She put her head back, closed her eyes, let the soothing sounds of Beethoven and Yo-Yo Ma wash over her. Alive and well, young, part of a team, plenty of future prospects; coming from her family, going home with her man. Wasn't much more you could ask for on Christmas, was there?

Jake Runyon

Most of the day before Christmas he spent driving around the city, and Oakland and Berkeley and the other East Bay cities, familiarizing himself with streets and neighborhoods. Early dinner in a Chinese restaurant on Taraval: egg rolls and mooshu pork. Back to his apartment building before seven.

A family party was going on in one of the other units — Yuletide music, laughter, kids' happy squealing voices. The sounds followed him upstairs, penetrated the walls faintly once he was inside.

He checked his answering machine. No messages. There hadn't been any messages since before last Saturday. He stood for a time looking down at the phone, listening to the distant pulse of music and laughter from below. Then he caught up the receiver, tapped out Joshua's number.

Recorded voice. But a different one this time, computer-generated, telling him that the number he had called was no longer in service.

Had his number changed. And the new one would be unlisted.

Runyon went into the bedroom. The silver-framed photo of Colleen, the best of the batch taken by a commercial photographer a few years ago, was on the nightstand. He brought it out to the living room, put it on the table next to the couch. Then he flipped on the TV, did some channel surfing until he found an old movie — always old movies on cable-system TV, even on Christmas Eve. This one was *Christmas in Connecticut*, with Barbara Stanwyck and Sydney Greenstreet, just starting. He watched it all the way through, not even bothering to mute the commercials. The party below was over by then; even the rain had stopped and the wind was quiet outside. Silent night.

He watched another film, something from the thirties with Bette Davis. When that was over he darkened the set. In the kitchen he took down the bottle of Wild Turkey, poured a thimbleful, carried the glass back to the couch. The table lamp illuminated Colleen's smiling image, oddly as if the glow were coming from within. He looked at it for a long time, holding the glass of whiskey, remembering Christmases with her in their Seattle home, one up in Calgary, another at a ski lodge. Presents they'd given each other, trees they'd trimmed, food and drink and special moments they'd shared.

He raised the glass. Aloud he said, "Always," and drank.

In the silence he sat there looking through more good memories, as if he were turning the pages of an album. Dwelling in the past so he wouldn't have to think of tomorrow.

Bill

The best thing about Christmas morning was the look on Emily's face.

She'd been happy the night before, all smiles after she finished reprising the three pageant carols in her sweet voice and Kerry and I gave her a literal standing ovation. But today, standing in front of the lighted tree in her robe and slippers with Shameless cradled in her arms, peering down at the array of presents we'd set out while she was asleep, she seemed radiant. Almost angelic in the shaft of pale sunlight, the first sunlight we'd seen in ten days, that slanted in through a part in the drapes.

"Some pile of loot, huh?" I said.

"Wow. Santa was good to us this year."

"I thought you didn't believe in Santa."

"I do now," she said.

I was basking in her glow when the cat did his perverse feline thing, jumping out of her arms and launching himself onto my lap from ten feet away. I wasn't ready for it and didn't get my hand out of the way in time; one paw smacked into my bandaged finger and sent shooting pains up my arm.

"Merry Christmas to you too, cat."

The lingering throb put Tuesday afternoon back into my thoughts. I shoved it out again, but not before I remembered Tamara looking at the smashed chandelier and saying, "Place'll never be the same again." She was right, and not just because of the chandelier. We'd counted five bullet holes in the walls and ceiling, and there was what would likely be a permanent bloodstain on the floor where Thomas Valjean's broken nose had leaked. There was also a leftover aura of violation and violence. It wouldn't be easy to work there now. Not for Tamara and me, anyway.

Well, why should we have to? We'd out-grown the place as it was, with the addition of Jake Runyon; a larger space, a better address with more modern, upscale trappings would be beneficial for business and morale both. We could afford it, we were on a monthly rental basis rather than a lease, and it was almost the end of another year. New year, new start. Tamara would be all for it, and Runyon wouldn't care, so why not?

Kerry came in with a breakfast tray. Hot chocolate for Emily, coffee for us, croissants, Christmas cookies she'd baked herself. When she set the tray down she saw me rubbing my knuckle, but she didn't say anything. She hadn't said much about Tuesday, other than "Thank God none of you were hurt" and "You manage to get yourself into the damnedest situations even when you're not working at it." Runyon and Tamara and I had downplayed the incident to the media; I'd downplayed it to Kerry and really downplayed it to Emily. Nobody but the three survivors knew just how close we'd come to dying that day. Maybe Kerry suspected it and maybe she didn't. In any case she had the good loving grace to keep her thoughts to herself and let me do the same with mine.

We dug into the food and drinks. Then we dug into the pile of presents. Emily squealed when she unveiled her state of the art, AT&T model 3360 cell phone with the vesuvius red faceplate; ran over and kissed me and kissed Kerry. I got another kiss when Kerry opened her package of French perfume.

As the family patriarch, or maybe as its oldest and only male member, I got to open my two presents last. Emily's was a ceramic sculpture she'd made in her crafts class at school; she said it was an egret and I took her at her word, but I would've loved it if it had been a cockroach. And Kerry's was —

A cell phone.

Emily let out a little whoop. "It's a Nokia, just like mine. Only basic black."

"His and hers," I said. "Now we can both be noisy in public."

"Cool! That is so cool."

I looked at Kerry. She shrugged and said, "Well, you must be the hardest man in the world to buy for. Besides, now you won't have to hang out in parking garages."

She moved closer, and I put my arm

around her. Emily came over and snuggled on my other side. Pretty soon she said, "This is the best. The best Christmas ever."

Best Christmas ever for me, too. One to cherish, to be thankful for. A special Christmas for a very lucky man.

About the Author

Bill Pronzini, recipient of the Lifetime Achievement Award for the Private-Eye Writers Association of America and three Shamus Awards for crime fiction, is the author of twenty-seven "Nameless Detective" novels, including *Boobytrap*, *Crazybone*, and most recently, *Bleeders*. He lives in Northern California.

8.29